WINTER GARDEN

WINTER GARDEN

BERYL BAINBRIDGE

GEORGE BRAZILLER
New York

Published in the United States in 1981 by George Braziller, Inc.
Originally published by Gerald Duckworth & Co. Ltd., London

George Braziller, Inc.
One Park Avenue
New York, NY 10016

Library of Congress Cataloging in Publication number: 80-70841

ISBN: 0–8076–1011–9

Printed in the United States of America

For Brian McGuinness

1

One morning early in October, a man called Ashburner, tightly buttoned into a black overcoat and holding a suitcase, tried to leave his bedroom on the second floor of a house in Beaufort Street. It was still dark outside and he had switched on the light. Hovering there, unable to take that foolhardy step on to the landing, he heard the whine of the filament; any moment the bulb would give out. Thinking of the blackness to come, he said, 'Are you sure you'll be able to manage?'

His wife, propped on pillows in the bed, struggled to keep her eyes open. She asked him, in a voice querulous with fatigue, what on earth he meant.

Though poorly phrased, Ashburner had thought it a reasonable question. Throughout twenty-six years of married life, between midnight and dawn, with the exception of his wife's two confinements, a funeral in Norwich which had obliged her to stop overnight and a three-day business trip he himself had made to Santander, they had never been separated. Inadequately he mentioned the coal that had to be brought up in a bucket from the cellar and the dinner he usually prepared for the dog at seven o'clock. 'There's also the possibility', he said, 'that the television set may break down.'

'It's only you that bothers with the fire in the drawing room,' his wife reminded him. 'And I'd be delighted if the television broke. You know it gives me a headache.' She closed her eyes. She was generally tired in the morning and always exhausted of an evening. 'You'd better hurry,' she urged. 'You don't want to miss your train.'

Ashburner began to have difficulty breathing. He remembered Nina's telling him that people with murmurs of the heart, not yet diagnosed, often adopted a crouching position. Cautiously he lowered himself on to his haunches and almost immediately pitched forward on to his knees.

'Have you gone?' his wife called.

'I'm tying on labels,' Ashburner said, and he reached up and clung to the brass rail at the foot of the bed as though to stop himself sliding into an abyss.

His wife's reaction to his sudden and peculiar need for a complete rest, arising so soon after their summer holiday in Venice, had been both sporting and unnerving. Ashburner hadn't wanted to be prevented from going, but he had anticipated a fair amount of resistance. Indeed, if his wife had played her cards right – expressed her opposition in some female manner, like bursting into tears – he would have abandoned his plans entirely; only a rotter would rush thoughtlessly off, blind to a woman's distress. But she hadn't objected. On the contrary, she had sent his old tweed trousers to be cleaned and fetched down his waders from the attic. Last Wednesday she had bought him a map of the Highlands. It had been her idea that he should leave the car at home and travel by rail. 'After all,' she told him, 'we both know how het-up you become when overtaken.'

'I can't deny it,' he said.

'And if you can't find a decent loch straightaway, or a suitable hotel, you can always hire transport.'

'That's sensible,' he agreed. 'I expect I shall be moving about quite a bit.'

'Two weeks in the open air,' said his wife, 'drifting in a rowing boat, will undoubtedly set you up for the winter.' It was true that severe blizzards were reported to be raging in the north of Scotland, but then he had never been a man to feel the cold.

8

If she had uttered one single word of reproach, Ashburner might have made a clean breast of things. Even now, when it was obviously too late, he longed to experience that same heady sensation of martyrdom which had prompted him as a schoolboy, accused of some group misdemeanour, secretly to approach his housemaster and claim sole responsibility for a breach in the rules.

'I may not be able to telephone you,' he said, hauling himself upright. 'There may not be a telephone.' His wife had slumped further down the bed and lay with both arms raised above her head, palms together in a diving position. 'On the other hand,' he said, 'you may be out.' According to Nina, his wife's posture, seeing that she wasn't on the edge of a swimming pool, was evidence of back trouble. 'And I'm not sure that I'll ring the office. They're bound to start pestering me. You'd better just tell them I can't be reached.' He thought he sounded insane.

His wife grunted. Ashburner knew she wasn't likely to dramatise his absence. Later in the week, when she met her friend Caroline for lunch, she wouldn't give the impression that her husband was in the first stages of a terminal illness or that he was heading for a nervous breakdown. She would simply say he had gone fishing.

'Well, I'll be off then,' said Ashburner loudly. He picked up his suitcase. It would be unwise to kiss her again. When he had done so earlier she had ticked him off for digging his elbow into her shoulder.

His wife remained inert. The covers had been partially pushed back as though she had intended to leap out of bed and perhaps make his breakfast. There were two roses appliquéd at the front of her nightgown, one on each breast. Ashburner was uncomfortably reminded of several things Nina had said to him less than a week before. She had remarked that it was clear, from certain observations he himself had made, that his wife lacked any deep awareness of

9

birds, of flowers; that she was innocent of theophanies, of mystical experiences, and those desired flashes of consciousness so essential to development. In short, she was a woman with no vocation for living. Since Ashburner had, to his way of thinking, been painting a fairly exciting picture of his wife, sketching in her sense of fun, her ability to spot an antique a mile off, her qualities as a mother, illustrated by the optimistic manner in which, during numerous rain-filled holidays on the beach at Nevin, she had sung *The sun has put his hat on*, he had been caught off balance. He could have kicked himself afterwards for not mentioning the extraordinary occasion when his wife saw her Uncle Robert, dead for five years, materialise in a bus queue at Hendon. Nor had he cared to mention the winter garden, a name his wife gave to the sunken yard behind the house, a paved area devoid of earth and so called because even in summer it lay as dark as the grave. Though his wife might have scored, poetically speaking, from the coining of such a phrase, he had known that Nina would immediately pounce on her choice of words and ludicrously interpret them as yet further proof of an abhorrence of sex. For different reasons he had kept quiet about his wife's habit, indulged in throughout the warmer nights of June and July, of stepping down into the winter garden with a skipping rope. To have hinted that his wife was trying to improve her figure, springing up and down in the moonlight, would have inflamed Nina. She was never consistent. She would doubtless have told him that his wife was shaping up to throw herself at anything in trousers. Of course Nina enjoyed needling him, and on this particular evening she had drunk almost two bottles of champagne; but in pointing out his wife's supposed failings, she had only exposed his own: he had never had any flashes, desired or otherwise, and his awareness of flowers was admittedly poor. In his view, as he told Nina, the things either poked up out of the ground or lolled in vases. Stung, Nina had gone further.

10

She had suggested that his wife was frivolous – all that laughing she apparently went in for at dinner parties and on the telephone.

At the time Ashburner had dismissed Nina's remarks as absurd, but at this moment, gazing down on his slumbering wife, bulky in her pink nightgown, he felt distressed. He wondered whether the night before, when he had made love to her, those slight tremors of her body had been due to stifled hilarity. He rammed his suitcase against the side of the bed. His wife fluttered one hand, encased in a blue cotton glove, in a queenly gesture of farewell.

Ashburner descended the stairs so forcefully that a shallow wardrobe, standing with its back to the skirting board in the hall, rocked violently. Its door, in which was set an oval mirror, swung outwards. He was confronted with an image of a face similar to his own, wobbling, as though reflected in water.

He went up the hall and into the kitchen to say goodbye to the dog. The dog, lying on its horse-blanket beneath the radiator, ignored him. Ashburner looked inside the knife-drawer for a pencil, thinking it would be a nice idea to scribble a note to his sons, and then remembered they no longer lived at home. Entering the hall once more, he side-stepped the wardrobe and pausing only to shoulder his fishing rod left the house.

11

2

Enid had hoped to arrive at the airport before the others. She'd planned to be sitting down when Bernard appeared. She wanted to be the one who would wave, call out, draw attention to herself. She was therefore flustered, having gone through passport control, to see Bernard almost immediately, sprawled on a plastic couch in the middle of the departure lounge, drinking out of a paper cup. Spread out on the floor in front of him was a collection of carrier bags. Nina stood behind the couch, leaning against a balding man who was clutching a fur hat to his chest.

'Got your bath plug, love?' asked Bernard, as Enid approached. He didn't bother to get up. He was wearing his old mackintosh and a pair of adventure boots threaded with bright yellow laces.

'Say hallo to Douglas Ashburner,' ordered Nina, as though Enid was a child at a tea-party.

'Hallo Douglas Ashburner,' said Enid, and she shook hands with the balding man.

Enid didn't know Nina all that well. Over the years they'd met at various dinners and at exhibition openings but hadn't ever been close. She knew Bernard very well. She wasn't sure how well Bernard knew Nina. Neither Bernard nor Enid had met Douglas Ashburner before.

As guests of the Soviet Artists' Union they had each been told they could bring a friend, at their own expense, or

12

husbands and wives if they wished. Nina's husband, the brain specialist, renowned for his remark that he'd never seen a painting yet that wasn't improved by a decent frame, was far too busy and successful to travel, and Bernard never took his wife anywhere. Enid wasn't married.

'I feel rotten,' said Nina suddenly. She swayed on her feet to prove it. Ashburner escorted her round the couch and sat her down beside Bernard. 'She doesn't look rotten, does she?' he asked, appealing to Enid.

'Not very,' said Enid. But she was aware that Nina, who normally carried herself like Joan of Arc at the stake, chin tilted as though she smelled the straw beginning to burn, was now slumped against Bernard, her head resting on his shoulder. Nina was famed for her beauty. Enid couldn't see it herself, but everyone else saw it at a glance. Nina had bold blue eyes, black hair that she sometimes plaited and legs like a principal boy. She had never been known to lose an argument.

After a few moments Ashburner went off to fetch a glass of water. There was no room for Enid on the couch, so she stood there looking anxious. 'Is it her head or her stomach?' she asked, speaking to Bernard as if Nina was already in a coma. Bernard didn't reply. He sat there, pushed sideways by the weight of Nina, staring gloomily at the floor. He detested illness.

'Should anything go wrong,' said Nina faintly, 'please be kind to Douglas. He's a good man.'

'Of course,' whispered Enid, and gritted her teeth in case she laughed. Twenty years ago she and Nina had been at the same boarding school in Norfolk. It didn't mean anything. Enid had been fifteen at the time, and Nina was two years younger. They had never been in the same class. Even in those days the thickness of Nina's hair had distinguished her from others. In summer the mildest of breezes sent her panama hat sailing from the top of her head to bowl across the grass.

Ashburner returned with a cardboard cup full of water.

13

Nina sipped and sighed. No one could make up their minds whether it was a good idea or not to send for the St John's Ambulance Brigade.

'Probably not,' decided Bernard. 'We might miss the bloody plane. Think of the arrangements at the other end.'

The thought was sufficient to revive Nina, who privately regarded herself as leader of their little group. After all, she had been to Russia twice before: once to Leningrad with a party of students from the Slade, and again when she had visited Moscow for three days in her capacity as wife of the brain specialist. When their flight was announced she rose pluckily, though she clung to Bernard for support.

Ashburner, who had no hand luggage, was obliged to carry Bernard's paper bags. He consoled himself with the knowledge that he would have looked dreadfully conspicuous supporting Nina. As it was, if he was spotted by anyone it might just appear he was alone. The fact that this was Heathrow, not Euston Station, could, if the unthinkable happened, be put down to amnesia.

From the moment of arrival at the airport he had found himself in a state of increasing nervousness. He had greeted Nina too coldly; he had uttered the words 'Oh it's you', instead of clasping her in his arms. She hadn't understood his predicament, his inability to collect his feelings in the midst of such activity and bustle. Inside he had felt anything but cold towards her, though he had been taken aback by the clothes she was wearing. Nina had punished him by going on for at least ten minutes about some friend she was dying to see again in Moscow, a regular humdinger of a man called Boris Aleksyeevich Shabelsky. Ashburner had been stunned by the fellow's unpronounceable name and the realisation that she was dying to see anyone other than himself. Moreover she had bullied him into opening his suitcase. Several packets of nylon stockings slithered to the floor; he could have been mistaken for a commercial traveller. And now she was ill.

14

'I don't mind telling you,' he confessed to Enid, 'how worried I am. She's not talking off the top of her hat, you know. She's a very strong grasp of medical matters.'

'Has she?' said Enid. She had to stop herself from breaking into a run to catch up with Bernard, who was now striding through the hurrying crowds, one hand grasping Nina's waist as he propelled her forward in the direction of the flight gate.

'And she mentioned it earlier,' Ashburner said. 'At the luggage counter. She gave me some pills to put in my suitcase.'

'What did she mention?' asked Enid.

'About being under the weather,' explained Ashburner. 'She hoped I wouldn't catch it.'

'That was kind,' Enid said. Glancing at him, she was momentarily shocked to. discover that he seemed to have sprouted a quantity of glossy black hair.

Ashburner, searching the broadwalk ahead for a glimpse of Nina, was disconcerted to see that Bernard was dragging his left leg quite noticeably, obviously parodying his companion's infirmity. Seen from this distance he resembled an inebriated tramp; but then Nina herself, for some extraordinary reason, was wrapped in a motheaten fur that was coming apart at the seams. Why on earth wasn't she wearing the mink coat her husband the brain specialist had given her only last Christmas? Even as Ashburner watched, she reached up and pulled Bernard's ear. Clutching each other at the waist they stumbled towards Gate 23. Such intimate tomfoolery accentuated the gap between Ashburner and Nina. If he had behaved in a similar manner, depend upon it, she would have shaken him from her like a louse from a blanket.

3

In the queue for seat allocation, Nina was pale but upright. She looked at Ashburner in his fur hat and smiled heroically.

'Feeling better?' he said.

'A little,' she conceded, and turned her back on him almost immediately.

Ashburner was alarmed by her indifference. He feared there was worse to come. 'I do feel', he said, anxious to show his authority, 'that we ought to sit in the front of the plane.'

'I want to smoke,' snapped Bernard.

'I was thinking of Nina,' explained Ashburner. 'Besides, should anything go wrong, the back end is always the first bit to fall off.'

'In that case,' Bernard said, 'she'll need a fag in her hand.'

No one bothered to ask Enid where she wanted to sit.

Hampered by his assortment of carrier bags, Ashburner had difficulty handing over his boarding pass. When eventually he entered the aircraft and struggled up the centre aisle to the rear of the plane, Nina was already seated, positioned between Bernard and a man in horn-rimmed spectacles with a briefcase on his knee.

'Ah,' breathed Ashburner and stood there, undecided.

'Do get settled,' pleaded Nina. 'You're causing a blockage.'

It took Ashburner some time to stow Bernard's belongings satisfactorily in the overhead lockers. Pieces of charcoal and several tubes of oil paint spilled on to the lap of the man with

16

the briefcase. Bernard stared impassively out of the starboard porthole as though it was no concern of his.

'You're in my seat,' protested Ashburner, at last. Now that he was actually aboard, his rightful place was beside Nina.

'Sorry, mate,' said Bernard. 'Once down, I stay down.' And he slapped his leg obscurely.

Face mottled with annoyance, Ashburner joined Enid on the other side of the aisle. He had been warned about the man's rudeness. Bernard's first appearance on television, in a programme featuring his work, had been noteworthy. Standing in the back garden of his dark little house in Wandsworth, he had pointed graphically at an upstairs window and referred to his unseen wife as the first Mrs Rochester. He had called the interviewer a prick for confusing an etching with an engraving. He had answered every question with such evident overtones of commercial insanity, giving vent to a burst of insensitive laughter when describing the death of his cat, lost under the wheels of a corporation dust cart, that he had become an overnight celebrity. He was never off the box.

I can't compete, thought Ashburner. A man in my position has to mind his ps and qs. He muttered audibly enough for Enid to hear: 'What a nerve the man has!'

'He can't help it,' said Enid. 'He's had a hip replacement. He's got a steel ball-and-socket thing.'

Ashburner's cheeks glowed redder than ever. He felt as though he'd been caught throwing stones at a cripple. He leaned forward in his seat to attract Nina's attention.

The man with the briefcase nodded at him and smiled.

'Don't look now,' muttered Ashburner, turning to Enid, 'but that fellow seems to know us.'

'He's probably a member of the KGB,' Enid said, and she studied the emergency exit procedures.

She was dismayed by the size of the aeroplane, having expected something larger. She wondered if perhaps they were

17

being flown out on the cheap. She had travelled three times by air, twice to New York and once to Los Angeles. On each occasion she had enjoyed watching a film. Her head-phones had blocked out the noise of the engines and she had scarcely known she was flying.

'I don't like small planes,' she told Ashburner. 'I don't think they're as safe as big ones.'

'On the contrary,' Ashburner reassured her, 'they're safer. Think of all those fellows during the war, limping home on a wing and a prayer.'

He had just begun to tell her of the miraculous return of a Wellington bomber whose tail hung by a wire from the fuselage, a story he'd come across in *Reader's Digest* while waiting for a dental examination, when the aircraft began to roll along the tarmac.

Enid bent over her knees and stuffed her fingers in her ears.

Nonplussed, Ashburner craned forward to look at Nina. The man in spectacles gave him a second, conspiratorial smile. Nina was talking to Bernard; sensing she was being watched she glanced over her shoulder. Ashburner was struck by the anxiety in her eyes. This woman loves me, he told himself, though many wouldn't realise it.

Nina fluttered her fingers at him, a gesture so reminiscent of his wife's dismissive wave of farewell that he was further cast down. Hurtling along the runway at a hundred and twenty miles an hour, he considered the probability that at this very moment his wife was unbolting the back door of their house to let the dog out to do its business. The sickening wrench he experienced when the plane left the ground and climbed into the sky made his heart pound in his breast. It wasn't only the ground he was leaving. It came to him in one of those flashes so often described by Nina, that his wife saw him in much the same light as the dog, a creature so dependable and infirm as to be thought incapable of straying beyond the confines of the winter garden.

Ashburner ached to confide in someone and had to wait fifteen minutes before Enid removed her fingers from her ears.

'Are we up?' she asked. She refused to look out of the porthole.

'Well up,' said Ashburner. He ferreted in his mind for the right words. 'I haven't known Nina very long,' he began. 'I expect you know her better than I.'

'Hardly,' said Enid. 'We're not intimate.' Now that Ashburner had taken off his fur hat she thought he looked like a troubled baby. It had something to do with the firmness of his pink cheeks, and his round, puzzled eyes.

'But you're in the same line ... art and that sort of thing.'

'Nina's gone into lumps of metal,' Enid said. 'I work mainly in oils.'

'But', persisted Ashburner, 'you do know her.'

Enid was often underestimated. Her pleasant smile and unremarkable features made her appear neutral. She had been made a prefect at school, and the subsequent discovery that she had cheated in the maths exam had caused astonishment. 'I've never been to Nina's house for dinner,' she said, 'if that's what you mean. Or to her cottage in the country, or to her studio in Holland Park. But once I had a long chat with her husband about India. He's keen on rugs.'

'Ah,' said Ashburner and fell uncomfortably silent.

He too had never been to Nina's house for dinner. He had, however, visited it in his lunch hour without being offered a morsel of food. Instead, Nina had encouraged him to make love to her standing up in the kitchen. 'Just get on tip-toe,' she had urged, 'and lean against the door.' It was in case her husband the brain specialist came home unexpectedly. Buttocks perilously close to the brass knob of the door, his transports of love had been tinged with theatricality. It wasn't quite the real thing. He found it terribly difficult to keep his balance, and his knees trembled violently. He wasn't a fit man, being overweight, and the muscles in his calves seemed

19

to have wasted away; if he had fallen on top of her the
consequences could have been fatal. Nina was quite right of
course: it would have been in bad taste to cavort in the
marriage bed, and it was bad luck that the sofa in her living
room was upholstered in velvet. There was a leather couch in
one of the consulting rooms on the ground floor, but mostly
the door was kept locked. Ashburner had suggested they line
the sofa with a protective layer of newspapers, but the idea –
and who could blame her? – hadn't appealed to Nina. He was
fearful, to the point of paralysis, of discovery. Nina usually
stripped below the waist but insisted he retain his trousers.
Such a welter of cloth and dangling braces rendered him
helpless. Had Nina's husband returned – apparently he was in
the habit of rushing home quite gratuitously for a ham
sandwich – Ashburner would have been hurled forward on to
the scrubbed pine table, ready for carving. Nina herself
pretended to require that added edge of danger. She told him
a ridiculous story about D.H. Lawrence who, disguised as a
character in one of his novels, actually made love to a lady
called Clara on a railway line. 'We should do it in all sorts of
places,' Nina had cried, remembering something else she had
read. 'In shop doorways and on the tops of buses.' 'Perhaps,'
Ashburner had replied doubtfully. He knew for a fact that
Nina hadn't used public transport for at least ten years. All *he*
required was a decent mattress. If she had truly wanted him to
give her pleasure she would have arranged things differently,
he felt. He had come to this conclusion on the frantic occasion
when, imagining she heard footsteps climbing the stairs, Nina
had manhandled him into the lobby and thrust him inside a
fitted cupboard near the door. As it happened, it had been a
false alarm; but, cowering there, his bare knees pressed
against the brain specialist's summer overcoat, a faint smell of
anaesthetic clinging to the fabric of the collar, Ashburner had
been frightened enough to become introspective. In this sort of
affair, he had realised, there was always someone who loved

and someone who played the clown, and possibly they were the same person. She takes me for granted, he'd thought. It's not a thing a man can tolerate.

'When we took off,' he observed sadly to Enid, 'he held her hand.' He looked sideways in the general direction of Bernard. The man with the briefcase, a miniature bottle of vodka at his elbow, raised his glass ingratiatingly.

'It doesn't mean much,' said Enid, though she didn't like to be told. 'Neither of them likes flying.' An hour ago she had cherished the illusion that it would be she who sat beside Bernard, shoulder to shoulder, as they were hauled upwards through the clouds.

'His nails are filthy,' Ashburner said. 'Quite indescribable. He must have mended a puncture on the way.'

'Inks,' informed Enid. 'You can't avoid it if you're etching.' She would have liked to sleep, but people kept handing her trays of food and offering her drinks. It was like being in a hospital ward.

21

4

Ashburner had once been interviewed on the radio, from a prepared script, about an explosion in the North Sea and had felt throughout that his chin was welded to his chest. For the life of him he couldn't look up. He'd been able to continue only by thinking that he would treat himself, later, to a pickled onion.

He was in the same agonising position now, head lowered as he read the duty-free list over and over, hemmed in by Enid, who was dozing, and the man on the other side of the aisle who, during the last quarter of an hour, had added winking to his repertoire of nodding and smiling.

When Nina had first suggested that Ashburner accompany her to Moscow, she had jokingly remarked that it might be better if he kept quiet about what he did for a living; he wouldn't want the Russians to think he'd come to spy on their shipping fleets in the Baltic. If asked, she said, perhaps he ought to imply that he was an engineer or a banker. He hadn't liked the idea. He wasn't any good at lying, and besides, as he told her, the particulars of his profession were quite clearly stated on his passport. Moreover he suspected, from what he read in the newspapers, that his background had been thoroughly investigated without his knowing. He had nothing to hide from the Russians apart from the fact that he was a family man. They would surely not hold it against him; he gathered that the Communists had practically invented free love.

The chap on his right was far more dangerous than a member of the KGB. He was one of those hearty and gregarious men who, if left alone even for a short while, behaved as though they were drowning. He would cling to Ashburner as to the proverbial straw. Given the slightest opportunity he would strike up a conversation; within two minutes he'd be babbling for an exchange of telephone numbers.

Ashburner had just made up his mind to raise his head and, if spoken to, administer some form of snub, when the man, still clutching his briefcase, left his seat. His departure exposed a perturbed-looking Bernard and the back of Nina; she was holding on to his arm as though to restrain him. Ashburner distinctly heard Bernard exclaim 'Bloody hell', followed by the words, sarcastically spoken, 'Thanks for telling me.' Then he too rose to his feet and limped up the aisle.

Seizing his chance, Ashburner sat beside Nina. 'I'm just on my way to the loo,' he said, in case he wasn't welcome.

'Sweetheart,' mumured Nina, 'I'm sorry not to be with you. It's your own fault. You spent so long faffing about.'

'I wasn't faffing,' he protested. 'I had all those wretched bags to carry.'

Nina called him a poor lamb, but he could tell she wasn't concentrating. She had folded her coat across her knees and was fretfully tearing small holes in its already bedraggled lining. 'Will I see anything of you?' he asked. 'I suppose you'll be kept pretty busy looking at Art.' He meant during the days ahead. He had such expectations of the nights that he couldn't bring himself to speak of them.

'You'll be coming with us. You'll have to,' she said. 'They won't let you loose on your own.'

'I don't think you ought to do too much,' Ashburner told her. 'Not in the day. Not until you feel completely up to it. I don't mind admitting that you looked more than a little seedy

23

down below.' Instantly he wondered whether he shouldn't have chosen a different adjective to describe her appearance at the airport. She was easily offended.

'Have you ever thought about illness?' she asked. 'Really thought. I mean, some people are ill and show it and others are ill and it's not apparent. Not even to them. Do you see what I'm getting at?'

'Not altogether,' he said.

'It's almost, Douglas, as if one only knows one is ill when told so by a doctor.'

'If one was run over,' said Ashburner, 'one wouldn't need to be told.' Nina herself at the age of ten had been knocked from her bicycle by a hit-and-run driver. She had a small, star-shaped scar on her forehead to prove it. He liked talking to her about medical things; she was extremely interesting when it came to brain tumours.

'You mustn't worry about my health,' she said. She touched his face with the tips of her fingers. 'I nearly wept when you fetched that water for me. It was so damned thoughtful.'

'Shall I order champagne?' cried Ashburner, dazzled by her big blue eyes seen at such close range, brimming with appreciative tears. If at that moment the aircraft had gone into a downward spiral he doubted he would have noticed anything out of the ordinary.

'I mustn't drink,' said Nina quickly. 'There'll be plenty of time for that later. The Russians are tremendous drinkers. Anyway, Bernard's consuming enough for all of us.'

'I didn't care for his swearing at you,' confided Ashburner. 'Even if he has got a gammy leg. I couldn't help overhearing.'

'It's not what it seems,' said Nina. She enquired how he was getting on with Enid.

He said Enid seemed awfully nice.

'Don't be taken in,' warned Nina. 'She's not a hundred per cent honest.' She didn't pursue the subject. Instead she mentioned that Bernard thought Ashburner had a very strong head, that his bone structure was compelling. There was also something about the set of his ears and the height of his forehead. What a stone carving he would make!

'Good Lord,' smirked Ashburner, curiously pleased. He stared bashfully out of the porthole and saw nothing save a circle of blue sky and some wispy clouds. It was so spacious up here and so crowded below. These days it was no longer safe to cross the road. Several days before a cleaner in the office had been mown down by a bus. He realised suddenly that if in his absence a similar thing happened to his wife, there would be no means of contacting him. They would put out an SOS on the wireless, but he wouldn't be available to hear it. At enormous cost to public expenditure country policemen in panda cars would motor the length of the Highlands. If she was injured tomorrow she could be dead and buried by the time he returned. He was so shaken at the thought that his lips trembled.

'What's wrong?' demanded Nina. 'Are you full of regrets?'

'What a ridiculous question,' he said evasively.

'You are happy, Douglas? Really happy?'

'Need you ask?' he said. It was unlike her to bother about his state of mind, and saddening that he couldn't match her mood. He would have given anything in the world not to feel responsible for his wife.

He had what was intended to be a friendly word with Bernard when he met him coming out of the lavatory. 'Look here,' he began, 'earlier on you must have thought I was queer –'

'Oh, I wouldn't go that far,' said Bernard, and he stumbled moodily past Ashburner and went back to his seat, his head wreathed in tobacco smoke.

Half an hour before they landed, Enid noticed something odd. The pilot announced over the tannoy that they were flying across the Soviet border; if the passengers cared to look below and a little to the left, land could be seen. Almost

25

everyone peered out of the appropriate windows and uttered noises of astonishment – everyone, that is, except Enid, who was fearful of disturbing the balance of the plane, and the man on the other side of the aisle, who was leaning back in his seat, mouth open and eyes closed. The odd thing was that though he held his arms in a cradling position his briefcase had gone.

5

They climbed off the plane and into a yellow bus without seats. It was snowing outside. A soldier carrying a rifle marched up and down beyond the windows. Soon the glass steamed over and they couldn't see him any more. Nina said at least three times: 'We're here. This is Mother Russia. We're here.'

They stood pressed against each other for a long while before the bus began to move. Ashburner once more was laden with carrier bags; according to Nina, cold weather had a diabolical effect on Bernard's hip. Ashburner resolved at the first opportunity to buy some sort of hold-all. If he was doomed to lug Bernard's painting equipment across Mother Russia it would be done in a more organised fashion.

On arriving in the baggage reclamation area they were approached by a young woman wearing a green cloth coat and a headscarf. She was holding a sheaf of papers and spoke unerringly to Nina.

'My name is Olga Fiodorovna. I am your interpreter. Welcome, Mrs St Clair.'

After a second's hesitation, Nina embraced her.

'I know you,' said Olga Fiodorovna, warmly. Releasing Nina she turned to Ashburner. 'Mr St Clair, we are delighted to have so eminent a man return to us.'

'Ah,' said Ashburner, appalled.

'This,' explained Nina, 'is a colleague of mine, Douglas

Ashburner, and the gentleman in the mackintosh is Bernard Douglas.'

'I'm Enid Dwyer,' said Enid, backing away. She didn't want to be kissed by a stranger. Seeing her suitcase appearing at the end of the conveyor belt, she gave a little whoop of recognition and darted away to retrieve it.

Olga Fiodorovna declared that Mr Karlovitch was waiting beyond passport control to greet them; he was Secretary of the Artist's Union and a very nice man.

'How lovely, how lovely,' cried Nina.

She and the interpreter began a vivacious conversation. There was much gesticulating and outbursts of merry laughter. Nina's hair leapt on the shoulders of her fur coat as she tossed her head from side to side.

How dark and animated she is, thought Ashburner, who, until meeting her two years before on the deck of the Cutty Sark, had imagined his preference was for fair women with placid dispositions; he strolled away so that he could admire her from a distance.

Bernard was lolling against a pillar and staring impassively at the luggage platform.

'What colour is your baggage?' asked Ashburner. He supposed Bernard couldn't be expected to haul it from the conveyor, not without collapsing.

'Shit brown and flake white,' said Bernard. 'You're carrying most of it. I don't bother with anything else.'

At that instant Ashburner's fishing rod, closely followed by Nina's scarlet suitcases, slid down the ramp. A porter with a trolley was summoned. Olga Fiodorovna consulted her documents and prepared to shepherd the little group through passport control.

'My case,' Ashburner said. 'It hasn't come yet.' He pointed in some agitation at all the suitcases that weren't his.

The interpreter told him to have patience. She laid a steadying hand on his arm and they stood for several minutes keenly studying the conveyor belt.

'Perhaps,' she admitted at last, 'it has been left on the aircraft. Stay here.' And she ran energetically towards an enquiry desk.

'This is a fine how-do-you-do,' observed Ashburner. He turned to Nina for comfort.

She was unable to give him any and instead called him a fusspot. Being so friendly to the interpreter had exhausted her and she was beginning to feel ill again. She sank on to the edge of the trolley and fanned herself with a pink scarf.

Bernard remembered a friend of his who had lost an entire cabin trunk of new clothes on a flight to Karachi. When they eventually turned up two years later the crotches of all his trousers had been devoured by ants.

'How extraordinary,' said Ashburner. Privately he doubted that any friend of Bernard's had the price of a bus ticket, let alone of a journey across the globe. He couldn't bear to look at Nina who, in his moment of disaster, was openly yawning; nor could he help comparing her with his wife who, in a similar situation, though possibly berating him for imagined carelessness, would be standing at his side, a tower of strength. Daily, he had only to mention the uncanny disappearance of his gloves, an important telephone number or the keys to the car, and she could be relied upon to spring into action. Her powers of deduction were remarkable; he had often referred to her as his 'little Sherlock Holmes.'

It dawned on him that if his suitcase couldn't be found at once it was imperative it should remain lost. 'Tell that Fedora woman not to get in touch with Heathrow,' he begged. 'They might contact my home.'

'Tell her yourself,' said Nina.

'But she's a friend of yours,' he pleaded.

'I've never seen her before in my life.'

'She said she knew you,' shouted Ashburner, distracted. He looked at Bernard for confirmation.

'She meant in the wider sense,' said Bernard and, suddenly weary, he lowered himself to the floor and lay there, boots crossed at the ankle, arms folded beneath his head. Almost immediately three or four men, shouting brutally, converged upon him.

Ashburner, pursued by Enid who wanted to be helpful, approached the enquiry desk and cunningly tried to make light of his situation. 'It doesn't really matter,' he told the interpreter. 'Surely we can call back another time or even let sleeping dogs lie until we're ready to fly home again. I can manage perfectly well without my suitcase.' He laughed in a reckless fashion as though he was the sort of man who regularly travelled like a hobo.

'Please be sensible,' said the interpreter severely.

She sat him down and instructed him to fill in various forms in triplicate.

Ashburner kept repeating that it was all a waste of time, that he could easily buy a toothbrush and so forth when they reached an hotel. 'I really couldn't care less,' he cried, but he had grown pale and his hand shook as he unscrewed the cap of his fountain pen.

The interpreter went away to tell Mr Karlovitch what had happened to his guests. As she crossed the hall she was surprised to see the Englishman in the soiled mackintosh being marched in the other direction. After an argument, during which permits and documents were passed frequently from hand to hand, she obtained Bernard's release and led him to a vacant chair near the tea-bar. Subdued by his experience, he agreed to remain upright.

Enid stared anxiously in the direction of the arrival lounge and thought of the Secretary of the Artists' Union pacing the red carpet, the smile of welcome fading from his eyes. She told Ashburner that she was sure his suitcase had just been mislaid in another part of the airport. Perhaps it had fallen off a wagon and been temporarily buried under a fall of snow. It no time at all it would appear on the conveyor; she would keep an eye out for it.

'I don't mind telling you,' said Ashburner, 'that I feel pretty sick. I'm not saying that I can always put my hand on everything when I need it, but I've never lost anything like this before. It could have the most frightful repercussions.'

'But you didn't lose it,' Enid told him. 'You can't be blamed – and anyway, you're not the only one.' She indicated a fellow passenger who sat at an adjacent desk laboriously filling in forms. 'That man who was sitting next to you on the aeroplane has lost his briefcase.'

It was of no interest to Ashburner. He knew he wouldn't see his suitcase again, not until he returned home to Beaufort Street, where it would be standing in the hall, ransacked, its Moscow label torn from the handle to be later used in evidence against him, its contents of new pyjamas and nylon stockings and co-respondent underpants in lurid and assorted colours strewn across the doormat. God knows what his wife would make of the several bath plugs, complete with lengths of chain, wound about his waders. Would she weep or rant? Either way he wouldn't have a leg to stand on. If she chose to rave at him there'd be no nonsense about keeping her voice down for the sake of the neighbours. He would stand propped against the wardrobe like a dead twig, the sap squeezed from him, waiting for the moment when she would snap him in half. If she cried, he would drown, sunk by his own philandering. Eventually she'd take herself off to her friend Caroline's. She would also take, after a judicious interval, his house, a third of his income and almost certainly the car.

'If it's any comfort to you,' said Enid, disturbed by the expression on his face, 'I think you're being very brave. I'd hate to lose all my little bits and pieces.'

When Olga Fiodorovna came back she was carrying half a dozen tulips on abnormally long stems. She presented them to Ashburner and told him that Mr Karlovitch had a deep

31

sympathy for him and that he mustn't worry any more. The Artists' Union would locate his suitcase. Now they must go to the hotel, and further enquiries could be made in the morning.

'How very kind,' murmured Ashburner. He trailed behind her, holding the flowers awkwardly in his fist. Due to the length of their stems and the weight of their full-blown heads, forcibly grown and streaked with yellow, the tulips rolled in all directions and finally hung down, pointing at the floor. It was as though Ashburner had just eaten a particularly large banana and hadn't yet thrown away the peel.

'Are you all right?' inquired Enid.

'Resigned, perhaps,' said Ashburner. 'It's out of my hands.'

'*Que sera, sera,*' she said.

No one could be sure what time it was. They had been so long under the artificial lights of the airport building that they had become confused.

'Don't you possess such a thing as a watch?' Nina asked Ashburner.

'Certainly I own one,' he told her. 'But I can't wear it. I'm too full of electricity.'

Bernard wore a wrist-watch, but it was unreliable and he hadn't bothered to alter it on the plane because he couldn't remember whether they were supposed to gain hours or lose them, nor how many. Nina felt it couldn't possibly still be daytime. She had risen at six o'clock that morning, in the dark, and when she had stepped out of the plane it had appeared to be dusk. They had probably arrived at tea-time and now it was supper-time, though she wasn't in the least hungry. It had been altogether the sort of evening that had she been on home ground she would have terminated by winding up her alarm clock and going to bed. She bumped wearily against Ashburner as, preceded by Enid and the interpreter, they followed the luggage trolley.

Clutching his bouquet of flowers in one hand and his fishing rod in the other, Ashburner stared straight ahead. Now that he was on the move he felt less jittery. He could do nothing more about his lost suitcase; it was up to God and the Artists' Union to find it. Above all, he resolved to abandon any notion of prudence in his dealings with Nina. Those silver moments in the air, when she had stroked his cheek, were but a prelude to the golden hours that still remained. If he was returning home to calamity and penury, the next twelve days must be lived with all the fervour of which he had once been capable.

Bernard, who was walking at Nina's side, said something to her that Ashburner didn't quite catch. He did hear her shout 'Oh Christ' in response. They were always, it seemed, having mysterious little conversations that either angered or surprised them both, though in this instance he thought they were probably being rude about his tulips.

Trotting three abreast and starting to smile apologetically, they advanced to greet Mr Karlovitch.

6

They were driven from the airport in a black limousine suitable for weddings. Though introductions had been clearly made and hands grasped in friendship, it was obvious from the beginning that the identity of Ashburner was shaky. It was a question of his name, half of which was the same as Bernard's and the rest apparently difficult to pronounce, and of his misunderstood relationship to Nina. Mr Karlovitch, conversing mostly through Olga Fiodorovna, asked Ashburner, first if his missing suitcase contained any valuable instruments, and secondly, when they were driving through a landscape of birch trees piled with snow, what opinion he held of the engravings of Dürer. Both times, Bernard laughed aloud.

They were fortunate enough to glimpse, before the single-track road merged into a motorway with six lanes of traffic, several old dwellings built of logs, with one or two hardy old persons wrapped in rugs on chairs on the rustic verandas.

'How healthy,' cried Nina, and she asked Mr Karlovitch if many such houses survived. Mr Karlovitch was sitting in the front of the car, wedged between Bernard and the driver. He spoke English, haltingly, but at this first meeting wasn't inclined to use it. Small and square, with gingerish eyebrows perpetually raised in concentration under his grey fur hat, he wore a blue knitted scarf so tightly wound about his throat

34

that each time he swivelled in his seat to talk to the interpreter his eyes bulged in their sockets.

Olga Fiodorovna explained to Nina that, picturesque as they might seem to foreigners, Mr Karlovitch would assure them that log cabins were no longer to the liking of the people. Mr Karlovitch's father had been born in just such an *izba* in Siberia. There had been a stove of baked clay and at night the children slept on top of it. Outside the house was a river; the temperature in winter was sometimes minus forty degrees and for eight months of the year the river was frozen to a depth of six feet. No one would wish a return to such conditions. Centrally heated accommodation in blocks of flats was available for everyone at low cost. Mr Karlovitch himself was lucky enough to rent an apartment in an area that was considered desirable. Also, it was near his wife's place of employment.

'How marvellous,' enthused Nina. 'In our country too we have blocks of flats, though they are not always heated.'

'Except when someone sets fire to them,' said Bernard.

Nina told Olga Fiodorovna that she was interested in the women of Soviet Russia. She would like to know whether Mr Karlovitch's wife was a skilled worker. The interpreter leaned forward in her seat to translate into the ear of the Secretary. The car drove past an enormous billboard straddling the edge of the motorway, stamped with the portrait of a smiling and bare-headed Brezhnev; blobs of snow clung to his painted cheeks.

'For God's sake,' hissed Nina, speaking out of the corner of her mouth. 'Don't leave it all to me. Think of a question.'

'Has anyone seen my hat?' asked Ashburner. He couldn't believe he had been so careless as to drop it in the airport lounge. All through the interpreter's rambling account of somebody's father sleeping in an oven, he had been probing the back of the seating in search of it.

Nina called him the giddy limit. At this rate, she said, he'd end up stark naked with nothing to show but his fishing rod. They all trembled with laughter; even Mr Karlovitch, who surely hadn't understood.

This outburst of hilarity, continuing as it did for a mile or two, served to relax the English contingent. They now became high-spirited and unrestrained, conducting themselves like deprived youngsters on an outing who, having wound down the windows and sniffed the salt air, fancied the sea was just round the corner.

Olga Fiodorovna smiled and nodded pleasantly. She had had sufficient experience of foreign visitors to appreciate the eccentricity of the English. It was they who were the most likely to be subdued in Moscow, obediently visiting the museums selected for them, and the most capricious in Leningrad, skilfully giving her the slip in both the Winter Palace and the Hermitage. They acted either with courteous reserve or wanton familiarity and could be counted on at all times to know precisely where and when such differing modes of behaviour might be found acceptable. Every one of them, unlike the French or the Dutch who had no necessity for guilt, had encouraged her to believe that when they returned to England they would write her a letter. Not one of them, not even the famous baritone who had said he was in love with her, had yet done so. Despite this, she was aware that each insincere declaration, each false promise, was dictated by politeness. She therefore allowed Ashburner to beat her about the shoulders with his wilting tulips until, having reached the suburbs of the city, the car slowed to the kerb and stopped.

Bernard peered out of the windows and was depressed to see a penitentiary made of reinforced concrete, twelve storeys high, with icicles fringing the windowsills.

'Is this it?' he said.

Mr Karlovitch clambered silently over Bernard's knees and left the car. They watched him sprinting through the snow, and then the car drove on.

36

'Was it anything we said?' asked Enid worriedly.

Olga Fiodorovna explained that it was Mr Karlovitch's day off. He had merely come to the airport out of respect. Now that they had safely arrived he could go home and eat his lunch. He would return tomorrow in his official capacity.

'His lunch!' cried Nina. Astonished, they learnt it was early afternoon.

With Mr Karlovitch gone from the car, Olga Fiodorovna assumed control. She indicated to the driver that he must stop smoking at once; she released the window a fraction to let out the stale air. Such was her authority that Bernard, who had just taken out his cigarettes, refrained from opening the packet.

'Now,' began Olga Fiodorovna, 'you will want to know something of the history of Moscow. You will not perhaps realise that the Kremlin was built on the site of the camp of Prince Yuri Dolgoruky, grandson of Harold, your own Anglo-Saxon King who was killed at the Battle of Hastings in 1066. Here he built his citadel, which the boyars later strengthened in a vain attempt to keep away the Mongol Tartars. By the fifteenth century, when Moscow had become the heart of a centralised Russian state, the Kremlin had taken on the basic form you see today.'

'You speak such marvellous English,' said Nina. 'Where did you learn it?'

'Here, in 1812,' continued Olga Fiodorovna, 'Napoleon came and conquered, only to find that his victory was turned into tragedy and ignominious defeat. Here, in 1941, the armies of Hitler trundled to within thirty miles of the city and then, deflected, followed the Napoleonic road westwards.'

'What does she mean by *here*?' asked Ashburner. There was nothing to see outside the windows save an immensely broad street under a thin crust of snow and several nondescript department stores.

'The name Red Square,' declared the interpreter, 'has no

37

special significance. It simply means beautiful. In the naughty old days the square was a market place in which vegetables and serfs were sold. Now of course it is a place for processions.'

I'll have half a pound of tomatoes, thought Enid, and that fellow with the big shoulders. She began to giggle quietly.

'Are you able to hear me in the front, Mr Burns?' demanded Olga Fiodorovna, apparently speaking to Bernard.

He ground his teeth; having done his homework before he arrived, he was irritated by the history lesson. 'What does that say?' he asked, pointing at a row of black letters, six feet high, erected on the roof of a nearby building.

'Labour is glorious,' translated Olga Fiodorovna.

'Oh, a hospital,' said Bernard, and wondered if he was brave enough to light a cigarette.

Olga Fiodorovna told him that in this instance, labour meant work. In her country such slogans were an incentive to the workers. It spurred them on.

'In my country,' said Bernard thoughtfully, 'a slogan like that would be an incentive to violence.'

At that moment the car turned a corner and he saw ahead of him a butcher's lorry stacked with carcasses, ribs striped with frozen blood, and beyond the lorry the white curve of the Kamenny bridge that spanned first the canal and then the Moskva river. When he craned forward to look out of the windscreen, there about a hilltop was a constellation of giant stars, ruby red, wheeling across the northern sky, and beneath them a cluster of cathedrals and bell towers and palaces with golden domes. A high wall, primrose-coloured against the snow, rose above an embankment planted with fir trees.

'Look, look, look,' shouted Olga Fiodorovna, unnecessarily.

They drove past the Kremlin more than once. Ashburner, who had been almost on the point of sleep when she had cried out so triumphantly, feared that the driver was caught in a

38

one-way system and that they were doomed to go round and round forever, gasping their appreciation and wonderment until the cows came home. Olga Fiodorovna held his wrist in a vice-like grip as she indicated the battlements, the graves of the Brotherhood, the onion domes tethered like balloons above the turquoise towers. She dug her pointed nails into his pulse as black crows flapped upwards through the Christmas trees.

'Yes, it's awfully pretty,' he agreed, worn out by her enthusiasm as they drove up the hill yet again and circled St Basil's cathedral for the umpteenth time.

She even went so far as to tap Bernard on the shoulder because he wasn't gazing in the right direction. 'Look,' she commanded.

'I am bloody looking,' he bellowed, and closed his eyes directly. When he opened them again the car was drawing to a halt outside the Peking Hotel.

7

Something had gone wrong with the arrangements. Their reservations were in order, but their authorisation document couldn't be found. Olga Fiodorovna scattered her papers in front of the booking clerk. Every quarter of an hour or so a multitude of people stampeded towards the desk and she was swallowed up, to reappear again when the hordes had receded, a solitary, argumentative figure standing on tiptoe. The English guests sat on a narrow bench in the anteroom to the lobby and waited.

After an hour had passed the interpreter, noticeably tense, led them into the main hall and informed them that Mr Karlovitch had been telephoned but was no longer at home, and now she was trying to contact the minister for cultural affairs. The whole business might take a considerable time to sort out. It was a matter of the smallest scrap of paper imaginable.

She gestured towards the restaurant and suggested that they should have tea, but first they must remove their coats.

'I don't want to,' said Enid. The massive doors leading from the snow-filled street were constantly opening and closing and she was far from warm.

Nina said she must do as she was told. No one was allowed to go anywhere in their outdoor things. Not indoors; it wasn't permitted. She knew that from the last time she was here. The brain specialist had kicked up an almighty fuss about it, to no avail, and he was a man not often thwarted. She drew Olga Fiodorovna on one side and entreated her not to feel too badly over the delay. 'We British,' she assured her, 'are used to hanging around.'

'You are very kind,' murmured Olga Fiodorovna. 'It is not a good day for me. I have many problems, many things on my mind. It is not just a question of papers.'

When Bernard took off his mackintosh Ashburner was impressed by the suit he was wearing. It was made of corduroy and had a matching waistcoat. Of course the colour, being a pale and impractical shade of honey, was a bit on the arty side, but the jacket was extremely well cut. There wasn't a speck of paint on it. Ashburner himself was wearing his third-best office suit and school tie. He hadn't dared pack his best suit because his wife might have thought it an odd thing to fish in. If Bernard was going to strut about attired like a peacock, it was probably just as well his suitcase had gone missing. He couldn't compete. All he had to change into apart from a fairly decent pair of flannels was his old tweed trousers. Not that Nina was in any position to throw stones. Ashburner had never known her to dress so peculiarly. She was wearing a voluminous kind of blouse, badly creased, and what he could only describe as a kilt, complete with a large safety pin attached above the knee.

The interior of the restaurant was the size of an aircraft hangar and decorated in the Chinese style with oriental screens, a lacquered ceiling of scarlet and black, and numerous pillars entwined with writhing dragons. Though it was difficult to see into the far recesses of the room – the windows were heavily draped and the Chinese lanterns unlit – it appeared to be deserted save for a score of waiters, who for some seconds stared insolently at the new arrivals before disappearing into the shadows. Bernard and the women thought the restaurant was marvellous and said so. The colours, the gloom! It was a work of art. Ashburner didn't

41

know whether they were joking or not. In his opinion, which he kept to himself, the place was absolutely hideous and could do with a couple of coats of whitewash.

'Shall I go after them?' he asked, peering in the direction of the vanished waiters. He was parched for a cup of tea.

Nina advised againt. Perhaps it wasn't opening time yet. It would be best if they waited for Olga.

A sudden uproar was heard at the end of the room, and from behind a screen painted with butterflies thirty or forty men emerged, broad-shouldered and fierce-eyed, some wearing moustaches, all shouting and jostling against each other as they tramped noisily past the group at the table. Booting open the swing doors, they swaggered out into the hall.

'They looked very alive,' said Ashburner, when he had recovered. 'Do you suppose they're your average man in the street?'

'Lumber men, oil men, collective farmers,' Bernard said. 'Ukranians, Georgians, Armenians – take your pick. They're probably here on a convention.' He stood up.

'Where are you going?' asked Enid.

He didn't answer her, but began to pace up and down in front of the swing doors, slapping his hip at intervals.

'I keep thinking about my hat,' said Ashburner. 'I shall catch pneumonia without it. It's below freezing out there.'

'It was a nice hat,' Enid said. 'You suited it.' She watched Bernard go into the hall and then ran after him.

Ashburner wondered whether this was an opportune moment to discuss the sleeping arrangements. He realised it was too much to hope for that the Artist's Union might accommodate Nina and himself in the same room. Photostat copies of the inner pages of their passports had been sent off to Moscow weeks in advance, though it did seem that neither Mr Karlovitch nor the interpreter had studied them very closely. Perhaps they had been mislaid along with the authorisation papers. 'If we're not actually in the same room,' he said, 'do you want me to come to you, or would you prefer it the other way round? We ought to work out some sort of signal and synchronise watches.'

'We haven't got any watches,' Nina said. 'And we may not even be on the same floor. I'm certainly not scampering along any draughty corridors in the middle of the night. I still feel ill, you know.'

He was so filled with impatience and longing that all his movements became brusque and uncoordinated. He knocked a cruet to the carpet and held Nina's hand so tightly that she winced. He said silly things to her, such as that he'd take care of her and make her feel better. She leant her head on his shoulder and told him she wasn't making any promises. He was happy at the way she rested against him but alarmed at the prospect of a sleepless night spent waiting for her to summon him to her bed. He was nearly fifty years old and it had been a long day. He stared at a gilt dragon whose mouth belched lacquered flame, and stroked Nina's hand. Please God, he thought, let my wife be sitting in the warmth, not out driving in the traffic. He didn't imagine she'd bother to put a match to the fire he had prepared the night before. In her view, fires were dirty things, blackening the ceilings and contaminating the atmosphere. She preferred her central heating. All through his married life he had cut kindling and hauled buckets of coal. He didn't know why it was that the sight of flames leaping up the chimney aroused such feelings of happiness within him; it wasn't as if he were a miner's son. In the cottage on the beach at Nevin, when the children had been put to bed, he had twisted strips of newspaper together to make firelighters. His wife had stood in the open doorway and shaken sand from the bath-towels. He had listened to the slap of waves on the shingle as the tide came in, and humming to himself had fashioned his twists of newspaper and his lumps of coal into an almost perfect pyramid in the apron of the grate.

43

Even then, over twenty years ago, his hair had been receding; unlike the sea, it had never returned.

'About my hat,' he said. 'Do you think Enid's taken it?'

Nina sat up and looked at him.

'She did say she liked it,' Ashburner said. 'Being light-fingered, I don't expect she could help herself.'

'You seem to have formed a very low opinion of her,' said Nina, startled. He protested that it was she who had put the idea into his head by mentioning on the aeroplane that Enid wasn't altogether honest.

'She cheated at algebra, for God's sake,' cried Nina.

After an unhappy silence she informed him that she was going to see what Bernard was up to. She didn't want him unsettling Olga Fiodorovna. The poor girl had enough on her plate; she was having a terrible time with her Mamotchka.

Ashburner was sitting alone in the near darkness when a waiter approached and apparently demanded to know what was required of him. Improvising, Ashburner mimed drinking a cup of tea and munching a cake. He held up five fingers for the tea order, and three for the cakes. If the interpreter was also feeling unwell, as Nina had indicated, she probably wouldn't be hungry.

Enid returned and said that no further progress had been made: the minister for foreign cultural affairs was at his *dacha* in the country, the mongol hordes were still raiding the booking desk and Olga Fiodorovna was throwing down her documents like a grand slam at Bridge.

'I've ordered afternoon tea,' said Ashburner.

'Good for you,' said Enid.

He sat fidgeting in his chair, moving the cruet backwards and forwards across the white tablecloth. He thought the room was having a depressing effect upon him; he had never liked the dark. Worse, he didn't know what he was doing here, a man in his position. But then, had he been anywhere else he would most likely have wished himself back. A man of

44

substance could not, any more than a beggar, be in two places at once. 'I feel ridiculously homesick,' he confessed. 'Isn't that foolish?'

'Nina's been giving you a hard time, has she?' asked Enid.

'I don't seem to know I'm here,' said Ashburner. 'I mean, I know we've flown here and I'm obviously not at home, but I don't *feel* I'm here.'

'You are,' Enid said. 'I can see you. Just about.'

Ashburner began in a rambling manner to tell her of his departure that morning, how even at the last moment he would have climbed down, cancelled his plans, if only his wife had shown any interest in him, had boiled him an egg, had bothered to look at his face. He didn't want to sound disloyal or to make excuses for himself. His wife was a wonderful woman in every way, though it was possible she lacked depth. It hadn't mattered in the slightest when they were young; the last thing a man wanted to come home to was a woman with depth. But she had never had any flashes of consciousness and in his ignorance – he'd had a very conventional upbringing – he had thought that a good thing. Her attitude to him had changed after her Uncle Robert had left her a considerable sum of money. Always before she'd relied on him for her clothing allowance, little treats, lunch at Harrods with her friend Caroline. Not that he'd ever grudged her a brass farthing. He would like Enid to know he wasn't a womaniser. In her sort of game, mixing with artists and television personalities, it was all taken for granted and really he wasn't, cross his heart, against anyone behaving in any way they thought fit. It took all sorts to make a world. His own sons were living in a very liberated fashion and he hadn't anything against them apart from the fact that he was still forking out for their flats and clapped out cars and so forth. It was just that he was distressed at having turned out to be like everyone else. He was frankly disappointed in himself, and that made him feel negative about one or two things. There was no denying that Nina was a wonderful person. Possibly she was even more wonderful than his wife; but believe it or not, at this particular moment, sitting in this Black Hole of Calcutta, he began to doubt that he felt very much for her – not *felt*. 'If my wife had only opened her eyes,' he concluded. 'If she hadn't flipped that damned blue hand of hers as though she was warding off flies –'

'Has she got low blood pressure?' asked Enid.

'She wears cotton gloves in bed,' said Ashburner. 'She's very proud of her nails.'

Seeing Bernard and Nina approaching, he jumped guiltily to his feet.

'Things are looking up,' Bernard told him. 'Olga's phoning the Kremlin.'

When the waiter arrived with their order of afternoon tea it was something of a surprise. He had brought three carafes of water, eight glasses and several silver-plated dishes filled with caviar.

Enid poured herself some water and drank thirstily.

'I ordered tea,' said Ashburner apologetically. He could see that Bernard was disgusted.

'I shouldn't worry,' Enid said. 'It's vodka.'

Nina refused to drink. She said she was feeling pretty awful as it was. She thought Bernard and Ashburner shouldn't drink either: they were guests of a foreign power and they oughtn't to let the side down, not immediately. For some reason Bernard attempted to comply with her request, though he failed.

At six o'clock Olga Fiodorovna at last brought them the keys to their rooms. She had taken off her coat and headscarf and wasn't at first recognised. Everyone except Ashburner, who merely thought her a pretty girl, was taken aback by her aristocratic nose and the width of her cheekbones. She wore her hair in an Eton crop save for one strand of hair that was pushed back behind her left ear and fell in a curve to her chin.

46

Waving aside a carafe of vodka, she ordered a glass of iced water which, when it came, she drank languidly, holding the tumbler to her lips and sighing. She got on very well with Nina. Ashburner thought he heard her say that she and Nina had the same mother, which was patently absurd as he knew for a fact that Nina had been born at Westcliffe-on-Sea.

After ten minutes had elapsed, Olga Fiodorovna suggested they retire to their rooms and report downstairs for dinner at seven o'clock. Then the itinerary could be discussed, objections aired, alternative plans considered. They should have an early night; they deserved it.

'You most of all,' said Nina, patting Olga Fiodorovna's valiant arm.

Ashburner was so befuddled with drink and fatigue that he forgot to ask Nina the number of her room. He did remember her going up in the lift with him, because she said how splendid the lift was, how old, how ornate, and he offered to buy it for her. His cheque book fell to the floor. He also remembered complaining to Bernard that someone had stolen his bath plugs and Bernard telling him that it didn't matter, all he had to do was put a wedge of lavatory paper in the plug hole. He thought he had taken Bernard's advice and turned on the taps. Then he imagined he heard the sound of water spilling on to a tiled floor and woke to find himself lying on a bed in an alcove. Hardly recollecting where he was, he ran panic-stricken into the small bathroom and was astonished to discover that there wasn't a bath, merely a shower attachment placed behind a torn plastic curtain. He was sobered by the whole occurrence. He washed his face and hands and combed the clipped two inches of hair that rested like a slipped bandeau, ear to ear, on the back of his head.

When Bernard knocked on the door to fetch him downstairs for dinner, Ashburner thanked him for his thoughtfulness. He fully realised that without Bernard's intervention he might by now be in the hands of the police, secret or otherwise. He was grateful to Bernard and furious with himself for having behaved like an ass.

'Feeling all right, mate?' asked Bernard.

'Super,' said Ashburner, though truth to tell, when he trod the brown carpet which ran the length of the corridor, he fancied that it, not he, was moving.

8

During dinner a man with his trousers tucked into the tops of his boots and smoking a little paper cigar approached the table and spoke to Enid. Angrily, the interpreter waved him away.

'What was that about?' demanded Enid.

'The usual,' said Olga Fiodorovna. 'A man away from home, on business, his wife left behind. He wanted you to waltz.' And she shrugged her shoulders contemptuously.

It wasn't usual for Enid to be asked to dance. She sniffed the burning fragrance of the man's cigar and was annoyed that she herself hadn't been consulted. She had hoped Bernard might have noticed the episode, but he was hunched over his plate, drawing something on the back of the menu.

Olga Fiodorovna promised that in the morning they would go sightseeing; maybe there would be time to drive to the famous Ostankino Palace, notable for its botanical gardens and once the suburban estate of one of the wealthiest of Russia's noble families. It was so beautiful in spring when the bird-cherry bloomed; they must all return in the spring.

'Poor buggers,' muttered Bernard, thinking how irritated he would be if someone commandeered his semi-detached in Wandsworth.

Afterwards, continued Olga Fiodorovna, they would lunch at a very extravagant hotel, and in the afternoon they were expected at the studio of a famous artist who worked on the outskirts of Moscow. Between six and eight in the evening it had been planned that they should meet a famous metal worker at his home. The house he lived in, very old and prestigious, had once belonged to Count Nikolai Ergolsky. The following day they were to be guests at a luncheon given in their honour by the Soviet Artists' Union. Perhaps in the evening they would like to go to the Bolshoi Theatre.

'Mr Douglas,' she said, speaking to Ashburner. 'Do not think I have forgotten your suitcase. I shall make enquiries first thing in the morning.'

'I have the utmost confidence in you,' he assured her, and wondered if he ought to write his name down on a piece of paper for her to take home and learn by heart.

He took little part in the discussion that followed, dealing as it did with artistic venues. When asked directly for his opinion, he said it all sounded marvellous and he would go wherever anyone else wanted to go. He had a headache and it was difficult to hear what the interpreter was saying above the noise of the restaurant, though he gathered that Mr Karlovitch would be accompanying them to both Leningrad and Georgia. Mr Karlovitch, it appeared, was very fond of Tblisi; he liked nothing better than to lie on his back in the sun and make fancy sketches of the monasteries.

On a rostrum a band was playing. The Chinese lanterns which hung from the invisible ceiling trembled at the blare of the saxophone. For some minutes a young man dressed as a Cossack sang, in English, a selection of ballads made popular by the Beatles. There was a particularly mournful one about a *Nowhere Man* which Ashburner considered was meant for his ears alone. *Doesn't have a point of view, knows not where he's going to*, crooned the young man, *Isn't he a bit like you ... and me-e-e?* Ashburner tried to tell himself that at home there were places similar to this, but he knew it couldn't be true. He had been nowhere like it, not even as a young man on a motorbike. It was the people who staggered him, not his surroundings. They filled the cavernous depths of the dining room from end

50

to end, behaving as though they were extras in one of those continental films his wife pretended to love, eating with such abandon, gesturing so exuberantly, rising from the tables to dance with such corybantic fervour that he felt half dead. They had only to look in his direction and he was transfixed, caught like a rabbit in the headlamps of a car, the little sugar cake he was on the point of devouring arrested in mid-air. What an immense advantage they have over me, he thought, being so totally at home.

Ashburner left the restaurant before the others had finished their coffee. He was yawning so repeatedly from exhaustion and lack of oxygen that he had long expected Nina to make some withering remark. He told Olga Fiodorovna that he was worried about getting up in the morning. 'I have no time-piece,' he explained.

It had been on the tip of his tongue to mention that his wife often woke him with a cup of tea.

Olga Fiodorovna assured him she would leave a message with the night porter, who would arrange for him to be called at eight o'clock.

'I'm only two doors along,' Bernard said, helpfully. 'Give us a knock and I'll lend you my shaving tackle.'

Ashburner thanked him and said goodnight. He was careful not to look at Nina. To his astonishment she ran after him and took hold of his arm as he was about to step into the lift.

'You're not huffy, are you?' she asked.

'Certainly not,' he lied.

'You're not to come to my room, Douglas.'

'I don't know the number,' he said stiffly. 'Nor what floor.'

'But I might come to your room,' she said.

'When?' he cried, agitatedly. 'What time? What if I've nodded off?'

'I can ring you,' she said. 'There's a list of numbers pinned to the wall above the telephone. I'm not promising, mind.'

'As a matter of fact,' he admitted. 'I'm not awfully keen. I

51

feel pretty tired.' But the very second the lift doors had closed and he was borne upwards away from her he was wide awake and pitifully anxious to see her.

His room, which he now saw clearly for the first time, having earlier been in too distressed a condition, was small and meanly furnished with a single bed, a utility desk and a worn armchair. On the wall hung a picture of some trees in autumn. He didn't know if the hotel was purpose-built or yet another stately home that had once belonged to a nobleman; if the latter, he must be occupying the serf's quarters. The shower didn't work and he was unable to open the window. Since childhood he hadn't gone to bed with the windows closed. He pressed his nose forlornly against the glass and saw below him a broad, deserted street, the snow scored with the tracks of cars, and beyond, a great expanse of darkness unrelieved by stars. I should never have come, he thought, and taking off his trousers, shoes and jacket, he fell into bed.

He was asleep when the telephone rang. It took him valuable moments to locate the light switch.

'Hallo, hallo,' he called, even before he had picked up the receiver.

A man's voice, accented and excited, bid him welcome to Moscow.

'Who is this?' asked Ashburner.

'I am your brother,' shouted the voice. 'It is Boris. Listen to me, please. Tomorrow night there is an exhibition of Zamyotov's work in the People's Institute behind Bolotnaya Square. You will go there. I have fixed it all. Do not listen to them when they tell you something else is specified. Tell them to jump in the lake, yes? Beforehand there will be a lecture. Unfortunately I myself cannot be there until later. You will like the etchings, I think. Have you understood?'

'Who am I speaking to?' asked Ashburner, bewildered.

The line went dead.

It occurred to Ashburner, briefly, that he might have been

the victim of a practical joke perpetrated by Bernard, perhaps at Nina's instigation. But then, recalling the pitch of Bernard's voice and his slightly flat vowels, he felt it wasn't possible: the man was an artist, not an actor. Catching sight of the one item of luggage that still remained to him, he absentmindedly took up his fishing rod in its canvas case and placing it against his shoulder began to parade up and down. He hadn't cared for the stranger's tone of bullying confidence. *You will go there ... I have fixed it.* Only last week there had been a report in the *Guardian* about an innocent bystander from Manchester who had gone to some meeting or other behind the Iron Curtain and disappeared for three days. Ashburner's step faltered. Had he in fact been given a message in code? Was there not something sinister in the phrase, *Have you understood?* 'Steady on, old man,' he said aloud and throwing his fishing rod on to the bed put on his overcoat.

The corridor was empty. The buxom lady who had given him his key when he came out of the lift had evidently gone home. He knocked heavily and repeatedly on the door of Room 409. After an interval he heard a female voice, speaking in a foreign tongue, raised enquiringly. He ran back to his own room and locked the door behind him.

When he had gathered his wits he realised that Bernard must have meant Room 405. Consulting the list of telephone numbers that Nina had spoken of, he dialled the appropriate one.

'It's no use,' said Bernard, angrily. 'I've just about had it.'

'It's Douglas,' Ashburner said. 'Look here, something pretty odd's happened to me. I'd like your advice.'

'She's told you, has she?' asked Bernard.

'It wasn't a she,' said Ashburner. 'Listen, I don't think we should discuss it over the wire, if you take my meaning. I'll come to your room.' When he went out into the corridor again the buxom woman had returned and was sitting at her desk.

'It's four o'clock in the morning,' said Bernard. 'This isn't

Chelsea. They don't like you wandering all over in the middle of the night.' Despite the hour, he was fully clothed, though he was without his shoes and socks. He listened to Ashburner's account of his mystifying telephone conversation and seemed unimpressed. In his view it was probably a wrong number.

'You think it was meant for you?' exclaimed Ashburner. 'I hadn't thought of that. There was, of course, that reference to etchings –'

'It couldn't have been my brother,' said Bernard. 'I'm an only child.' At the sight of Ashburner's naked legs, incongruously showing beneath his winter overcoat, he started to laugh.

'Don't think for one minute,' Ashburner said, 'that I'm unaware of the opinion you and Nina hold of me. I even understand it. We come from different worlds, after all. I'm a shy man, I haven't had the advantages of a bohemian education. In the company of such people as yourself I play possum.'

Bernard was alarmed. 'Look, mate,' he said. 'I didn't intend –'

Ashburner held up an authoritative hand for silence before thrusting it inside the revers of his coat. Propelled by introspection, he walked napoleonically back and forth in front of the curtained window.

'Normally,' he said, 'I feel more or less at ease with myself. I've never been burdened with those complicated subtleties of thought that constantly assail Nina and others of her ilk. I find reality quite stimulating enough for my own needs. But I do bear in mind that everything depends on other factors. Why for instance does one sprawl on the grass in summer?'

'Search me,' said Bernard.

'Simply because it is summer,' explained Ashburner. 'It's a seasonal sprawling. I mean, if I were to run into the street now and lie face downwards in a snow drift, it would be considered eccentric.'

54

'Have you been out?' asked Bernard.

'It may interest you to know,' declared Ashburner loudly, 'that I can conduct a perfectly intelligent conversation with people in my own walk of life. I don't wish to sound offensive, but if for some reason you found yourself rubbing shoulders with colleagues of mine, it might be you who would be thought something of an odd ball.'

Better hang on, thought Bernard. The poor bugger is obviously beside himself with rage. It was all Nina's fault; she'd kept him dangling like a broken yo-yo since morning.

'Moreover,' shouted Ashburner, 'I happen to belong to a profession in which the words *Tell them to jump in the lake* could be of particular significance.' Having rid himself of this enigmatic statement, he leaned wearily against the window and closed his eyes.

Bernard could think of nothing worth saying. He sat on the edge of his bed and lit another cigarette. He wondered whether Ashburner sold outboard motors. Or was it possible that Nina had taken up with an undertaker?

'Made a night of it, did you?' asked Ashburner suddenly.

'Yes,' confessed Bernard, taken aback. 'We did have a few drinks.'

Ashburner frowned. 'I didn't think Nina was into drinking. Not tonight.'

'Who mentioned Nina?' said Bernard, recovering. 'I was with Enid.'

Ashburner removed a paisley dressing gown and several carrier bags from the armchair and sat down. A small bottle of pills fell to the carpet. He twitched the hem of his coat to cover the tops of his white knees and sighed heavily.

'You're absolutely right,' he said. 'I'm a fool. I'm out of my depth.' He attempted to grasp the bottle of pills with his navy blue toes. 'I suppose in Nina,' he admitted, 'I got more than I bargained for.'

'You could say that,' said Bernard.

55

During what remained of the night, Ashburner received four more telephone calls. The first was inconclusive because the moment he spoke the line was disconnected. The other three, commencing at a quarter to five and occurring at forty-minute intervals, acquainted him with the time.

9

The problem of Ashburner's missing suitcase threatened to take up most of the morning. There wouldn't be time to visit the Ostankino Palace as Olga Fiodorovna had originally suggested. Mr Karlovitch was unfortunately detained at the office and it wouldn't be advisable for the group to travel unattended. They would have to accompany her while she made her enquiries.

'You like to have a veto on where we go – is that it?' asked Bernard mutinously, though at this particular moment the only place he wanted to go was back to bed.

'You are quite free to visit any place you wish, Mr Burns,' said the interpreter, looking at him calmly. 'Without prior notification from the Soviet Artists' Union, or a similar body, you are equally free to spend all your time queuing for admission. It is minus twenty-three degrees outside. Please put on your hats.'

Neither Bernard nor Ashburner possessed a hat. Frowning, Olga led them out into the street in search of the car. They followed several paces behind, mincing along the slippery pavement and clutching at each other for support.

'It's not all that cold,' boasted Enid, who was wearing a swagger coat which had belonged to her mother and a cap with ear-flaps which she had bought at the Army and Navy Stores when she was a student. 'Sometimes,' she lied, 'it's worse than this at home.' Before going to sleep at night, she often read for pleasure Cherry-Gerrard's chilling account of the worst journey in the world, the dreadful polar trek north when it had blown so cold that the breath of sledge-hauling men froze to ice on their lips. In her warm bed she had shivered. Now she wondered if there hadn't been some exaggeration.

Olga Fiodorovna gave her a lecture on the differences between island and land masses. 'Your country is surrounded by water. If the temperature drops severely, you know about it quickly. Here it can appear deceptively mild until a complete stranger rushes up to you and pulls your nose because he can see it is getting frost bitten.' She turned and gripped Enid's nose between thumb and forefinger.

'Gracious,' cried Enid, and she fell back behind Bernard, her eyes smarting.

They had found the car and settled into it when Olga Fiodorovna uttered a moan of despair and ordered them out. For an instant they feared she had commandeered the wrong car or that the engine was about to explode, but it transpired that the interior was badly polluted; the driver had been smoking again. They huddled together at the kerb, waiting for the nasty smell to blow away. A party of infants, roped together for safety, enormously rotund in padded snow suits and scarves and woolly hats, tottered along the sidewalk. Enid chose to distribute sweets among the rear of the column. The children at the front, checked in their wandering stride, lost their balance and sat abruptly in the snow; keeling over like nine-pins, the kindergarten fell into disarray. The stricken toddlers, tangled in their guidelines and stoically silent, thrust mittened thumbs to their mouths and stared cheerfully at the sky.

'You've a way with children,' observed Bernard, as the car drove off.

Ashburner hoped he was being driven to the airport. He had stopped apologising for upsetting everyone's plans. The

58

contents of his suitcase, previously despised, had become precious. Wretched in yesterday's shirt, he had attempted to buy various toiletry articles at the visitors' shop on the second floor of the hotel. Though lights blazed above the counter and at least three women lounged behind it, he had been turned away empty-handed. Worse, Nina hadn't come down to breakfast. He had telephoned her frequently from the lobby, without success. Enid had knocked at the door of her room but received no reply. She's said that Nina couldn't be all that tired; they'd both gone upstairs to bed shortly after he himself had left the restaurant. Ashburner hadn't liked to pursue the matter further. Knowing that Enid had spent most of the night with Bernard, he could hardly ask her if she had heard Nina moving about in the room next door. Olga Fiodorovna, when told that Nina couldn't be roused, had said it would be best if Mrs St Clair stayed where she was. There was no point in disturbing her; they weren't going anywhere important. Inwardly, Ashburner disputed this. Nina could be lying seriously ill. To his shame, he was far too exhausted and unwashed to make an issue of it.

They drove through the white city, hurtling along avenues so broad that the pedestrians on the distant pavements swirled like black flecks in the snow.

'Stop,' shouted Bernard, suddenly.

He had glimpsed in the narrow gorge below the citadel the outline of a swimming pool. Steam puffed above the blue water and drifted into the trees. The driver, deprived of nicotine, accelerated and the car leapt on the icy road. Bernard, too choked for words, swivelled in his seat and pounded on the leather upholstery. Olga Fiodorovna gazed at him placidly and played with the knot of her silken headscarf.

'He had a bad night,' volunteered Enid.

Ashburner was comfortably dozing; now and then as the car bounced in its tracks a little snort of tiredness broke from his open mouth.

'I've got to get out,' said Bernard. He took hold of the handle of the door. 'I've got to use my bloody legs.'

Olga Fiodorovna looked anxiously at Enid, who explained that Bernard probably needed exercise on account of his funny hip.

Olga Fiodorovna leaned forward and placed her arm round Bernard's shoulder. She talked soothingly to him. She would make her phone calls to the airport and, while she did so, he and the others were at liberty to walk in the open air. Everyone must avoid gaining entrance to buildings, however historical and enticing. He personally must give an undertaking to be good and remain outdoors.

'Yes, yes, yes,' agreed Bernard, flinching under the chummy pressure of her arm and determined the moment he was rid of her to make for the swimming pool in the moat.

Some minutes later the car came to a halt beside the steps of St Basil's Cathedral. Helping Bernard from his seat as though he were an invalid, Olga Fiodorovna pointed diagonally across Red Square towards a large Gothic edifice, turreted and towered, situated lower down the hill. She stipulated that in one hour's time they should meet in the English bar of the Hotel Nationale.

'One hour,' repeated Bernard, thrusting his fists deeper into his pockets lest they should fly out and punch her to the ground. Normally a solitary man, he wasn't used to taking orders.

Ashburner, dragged from the interior of the car, staggered under the onslaught of the wind. He waved uncomprehendingly as Olga Fiodorovna was driven away. He was all at sea. Within seconds his ears turned purple, and so fierce was the pain that he shuffled on the spot like a tap dancer. Upon learning from Enid that Bernard wanted to go to some outdoor swimming pool, he was flabbergasted. 'My dear fellow,' he shuddered. 'You can't. The shock would kill you.' He looked wildly about him for shelter. Clutching his incendiary ears and calling for the others to follow, he jogged tormentedly up the steps of St Basil's.

Bernard walked off in a northerly direction. He saw no reason why he should enlighten Ashburner; he hadn't any intention of swimming, only of sketching the surroundings of the pool.

Cowering behind a stout pillar at the entrance of the cathedral, Enid and Ashburner watched his progress. But for a flock of pigeons he was alone in the centre of the Square. A line of people, plodding two by two, heads bowed, wound in a straggling procession about its perimeter. Directly opposite the cathedral the wooden doors of the Fortress opened on to a courtyard. A squad of soldiers, fur-capped and muffled from throat to ankle in top-coats of olive green, stood to attention on the cobblestones. Above them the golden domes burned in the grey sky. The soldiers, responding to some unheard shout of command, tramped into the square and advanced towards Bernard. Unaware that he was outflanked, mackintosh flapping, he limped onwards. Ashburner called his name. Alerted, Bernard looked back and faltered; attempting to run for it he slipped and fell on all fours in the snow. The pigeons lifted into the wind and circled above the square. The troops strutted past. Picking himself up and changing course, Bernard headed for the street. He raised his arm as if hailing a taxi.

'Better pretend we didn't see that,' said Enid, as they stumbled down the steps in pursuit. 'I expect he's in pain.'

Nobody could be sure they would recognise a taxi if they saw one. Ashburner thought taxis probably didn't exist; such things were surely out of place in an equal society. When a large white car stopped at the kerb he hesitated but then, nudged forward by the others and galvanised by the cold, clambered inside.

'Hotel Nationale,' said Bernard.

The car drove off so fast they all fell backwards in their

seats. Almost at once the driver held up his arm and rubbed his fingers together suggestively.

Enid was the only one who had any roubles. 'This isn't a taxi,' she whispered. 'There's no meter.' She was fearful they were being hijacked.

Ashburner didn't care what sort of vehicle it was; he would gladly have ridden in a cattle truck to be out of the frightful blast of the wind. His ears, previously frozen, now throbbed exquisitely.

They waited for two hours in the English bar before Olga Fiodorovna arrived. She had spent a banal morning holding on to the end of a telephone.

'Somewhere outside,' she said, gesturing towards the windows, 'people are conducting their lives in a simple, uncomplicated manner.'

Ashburner nodded doubtfully and fetched a chair to the table.

Telex messages were stuttering back and forth between Sheremetyev airport and Heathrow, she said, but as yet there was no news of his elusive suitcase. Ashburner's signature was required on several new forms. Her life, she implied, was a paper chase. Even so, she had managed to purchase some little commodities; taking from her handbag a toothbrush, a tube of toothpaste and a bar of soap, she laid them in front of Ashburner.

'I'm much more concerned about head-gear,' he said ungraciously, and began to question her as to where he could buy a fur hat or a cap with ear pieces and the relative prices of such items here and at home. It wasn't until Enid put her oar in and mentioned balaclavas, recounting a gruesome incident on the Polar trek north when sweat soldered wool to the head, necessitating medical treatment, that he remembered the absent Nina and cried out her name. His energetic rise from the table spun a dish of sweet gherkins to the floor.

Olga Fiodorovna said there was no need for alarm. At this

moment Mrs St Clair was lunching with Boris Shabelsky in the Artists' Union Club, once the home of Prince Nevsky, and afterwards she would be driven by him to her next appointment. This afternoon they would all be reunited in the studio of the illustrator, Andrei Petrov.

Reassured, Ashburner went into the washroom to clean his teeth. The paste lathered like soap and the brush disintegrated in his mouth. Spitting nylon stalks into the basin and examining his ears for frostbite, he dwelt on an image of Nina, blue eyes wantonly regarding her companion as they talked meaningfully about Art. This Boris character was obviously one of those clever chaps who spoke English; otherwise the interpreter would have been present. Perhaps Mr Karlovitch was chaperoning them. It's just possible, thought Ashburner, that she will mention me. Holding the remains of his toothbrush in one hand and still frothing at the lips, he ran back into the lounge bar and seizing Bernard by the shoulder exclaimed, 'Boris!'

'He is, I think, a friend of yours,' said Olga, when she had fathomed the cause of his excitement. 'He contacted Mr Karlovitch this morning and was most insistent that you should attend the exhibition.'

'I thought we were having tea with a metal worker,' Bernard said.

It was important, Olga Fiodorovna stressed, to realise that arrangements were flexible. A great deal of care had gone into the organisation of their visit, but if Mr Douglas thought fit to make alternative plans it wasn't in her nature to dissuade him.

'I'm quite in the dark,' protested Ashburner. 'I really don't know the fellow from Adam.' He felt in some undefined way that he was at fault and wished his wife was at his side. In company she had been known, once or twice, to back him up. He thought she might have found the exact, light-hearted phrase calculated to put Olga Fiodorovna in her place.

He was further discomfited during lunch to be handed an envelope containing a hundred roubles.

Olga Fiodorovna seemed annoyed when he argued that he wasn't a guest of the Soviet Union. 'Mr Douglas,' she said, 'You are destined to be awkward.'

Blushing, he pocketed the money. He felt like a kept man.

Later they drove to a tourist's shop to buy him a hat. Bernard refused to step inside. Shopping, he said, was anathema to him and he didn't want anything for his head. If need be he'd wrap an old newspaper about his ears. After a whispered consultation the driver was instructed to take Mr Burns to the artist's studio and return without delay.

Inside the store, Ashburner changed his mind. He was disinclined to spend eighty pounds worth of traveller's cheques on a fur hat which would have to be abandoned long before he arrived in Chelsea. He was forced to loiter in the wake of the two women as they wandered from counter to counter. Shocked, he examined his reflection in a mirror; his complexion flared pink and mauve. Far from resembling a stone carving he thought his face looked like something stamped on the lid of a biscuit tin.

At the last moment, when the car was actually at the kerb, Olga Fiodorovna, murmuring that she had business to attend to, turned back and was gone for quite ten minutes.

Ashburner, waiting in the car with Enid, dwelt on the events of the previous day. In the aeroplane Nina had asked him if he was happy, though she herself had looked rather miserable. But then, frankly, it had never been apparent that Nina had any capacity for happiness or that she appreciated it in others. In the restaurant she had told him to stop laughing, that the sound he was making was absurd. It was difficult to think of an acceptable way of laughing when she behaved so distantly yet lay so close to his heart, and of course he had been suffering from the effects of that unusual afternoon tea. He imagined the squeal, so repugnant to Nina, that had issued from his lips had been the result of repression rather than amusement. One way or the other, he had been repressed for the last twenty-four hours.

'I could wring Nina's neck,' he said. 'I really could.' He was astonished at the ferocity of this outburst.

'I know what you mean,' Enid said. She was thinking of the unobtainable Bernard. 'It would be more peaceful if she was dead.'

'Good God,' cried Ashburner. 'What do you take me for?'

'Or in prison,' ventured Enid. 'At least you'd know where she was.'

There was a second, unexplained halt when they reached the outskirts of the city. They drove into the courtyard of a block of flats. Ashburner, fancying that they had reached their destination, was maneuvering himself to follow Olga Fiodorovna from the car when she shut the door in his face. She turned once to look back, hand held up like a traffic controller, and then, silk scarf fluttering in the wind, ran across the yard. The driver took out his cigarettes.

'She's always on the go, isn't she?' remarked Ashburner, irritated by the high-handed manner in which the interpreter had departed.

'She's probably visiting her Mamotchka,' Enid said. 'She's having a spot of bother with her at the moment.' Enid herself had been bothered by her own mother for many years. 'I suppose,' she said, looking out at the bleak vista of concrete and snow, 'that you get on well with your Mum.'

'Not too badly,' admitted Ashburner. 'Though she's frighfully shy.' He was telling Enid how his wife still went down with raging headaches on the anniversary of *her* mother's birthday when the driver, who had been slumped contentedly in a cloud of smoke, sat up abruptly and stubbed out his cigarette. A car was nosing into the courtyard behind them.

'After her mother's death', said Ashburner, 'she perked up

65

for a year or two. She wouldn't let me go to the funeral. I sent a wreath of course. But then her Uncle Robert died and she became depressed again.'

'The uncle with the money?' asked Enid. The light was going from the sky. She watched as two men, one carrying a suitcase wrapped in canvas against the weather, passed the windows of the car.

'I don't understand depressions,' said Ashburner. 'Do you?'

'Only when my work's not going well,' Enid said.

Ashburner gathered she was alluding to her art; Nina often referred to her painting as work. 'I'm afraid I'm far too active to give way to it,' he said. 'I'm always doing things, mending sash cords, making fires.' But even as he spoke a peculiar feeling of lassitude stole over him. He peered out of the window of the car as though from the interior of a cave and had the greatest difficulty raising his eyes from the footprints in the darkening snow. A little church music would have reduced him to tears. He was far too worldly to imagine that his mood had anything to do with his separation from Nina. What I'm experiencing, he told himself, isn't unhappiness but fatigue.

10

The studio of the illustrator Andrei Petrov was housed in a five-storey building surrounded by trees and set beside a frozen lake. There was a bicycle shed in the grounds and the statue of a man bending down to admire a leaping fish.

The short journey from car to entrance hall was sufficient to chill Ashburner to the bone. In the lift he thought he heard someone groaning but it was merely the chafing of the ancient cable.

Olga Fiodorovna escorted them to the artist's door and then, explaining that she had visited Mr Petrov on numerous other occasions, left them. She didn't use the lift. They heard her running down the stone stairs.

The room they entered was more like an English bed-sitter than a studio. Though there was a couch, table and chairs, and a small kitchen half-concealed behind a curtain, it contained neither easel nor drawing board. A collection of cotton squares printed with koala bears, maps of Tasmania and kangaroos, some framed behind glass, some stretched on wooden battens, hung on the wall above the fireplace. The artist's wife, a motherly woman in a pinny, was cutting a chocolate cake into portions. When she was introduced to the visitors by her husband, her hand shook noticeably and she was too bashful to look them candidly in the eye. Andrei Petrov, though more confident than his wife, spoke with one hand partially covering his mouth as if he hardly believed what he was saying. The Secretary of the Union, Mr Karlovitch, was strolling in the grounds and would join them shortly. In the meantime he himself, with the limited amount of English at his disposal, would try to acquaint his distinguished guests with his work and aspirations: as could be seen, he wasn't only an illustrator but something of a connoisseur of folk-art. 'Them', he said, indicating the cloths above the fireplace, 'I unearthed in Sydney, Australia.'

'Charming,' Ashburner said.

Encouraged, the illustrator pointed to the table on which lay a small charcoal drawing of a child hugging a teddy bear. He said deferentially to Ashburner: 'That is the frontispiece of my latest book. I hesitate to show it to a man so forward in his field.'

Bernard was no help. He sat morosely in an armchair, balancing a plate of crumbs on his knee.

'It is for the six- to nine-year-olds,' elaborated Andrei Petrov.

'It's awfully good,' Ashburner said. He was to remember later the exact positioning of the white woolly rug he so thoughtfully side-stepped as he advanced across the polished wooden floor.

On his return to the Peking Hotel he immediately telephoned Nina's room. As he had expected, he received no reply. There wasn't any point in his going upstairs; he had nothing to change into and his shower didn't work. Disturbed, he prowled the lobby, buffeted by numerous women who, swaddled in furs, waited in a disorderly queue for the services of the cloakroom attendant. It was impossible for Ashburner to tell to which class they belonged. If he had been at home he might have referred to them as day trippers; his own wife, in winter, beyond a faint reddening of the nostrils, remained inescapably Kensington. Divested of hats and coats and scarves, the women emerged several inches thinner though

68

still formidably stout-busted in layers of brightly coloured jumpers worn above minuscule skirts. It wasn't surprising, he thought, that there had been an October Revolution: really cold weather was a great leavener of society. It was also possible that arctic conditions affected people in much the same way as heat waves; the Secretary of the Union had certainly behaved very oddly, going for a stroll in sub-zero temperatures, but perhaps that had something to do with his Siberian background.

Entering the restaurant and choosing a table nearest to the swing doors, Ashburner took from his pocket the large brown envelope Mr Karlovitch had given him earlier. Opening it, he draped Nina's pink scarf across his knee and read her note again. *Sweetheart, wear this and keep your little old head warm in memory of me. See you when you get back.* Though she had never written to him before the levity of her message struck him as characteristic. It was the wording of the last sentence that he found peculiar. How convenient that she had happened to have a large envelope handy. Picking up the scarf he held it to his cheek and was sitting in this vulnerable attitude when Bernard came into the restaurant.

'Listen, Douglas,' Bernard said. 'I've been up to her room and she's not there. I'll tell it once more and then leave me alone. I've just about had it.'

'I don't need to hear it again,' said Ashburner. 'I know your side of it.' He folded both note and scarf and stuffed them in the pocket of his jacket. 'But just answer me this if you can. Why did Olga say there was no need to disturb Nina this morning when she already knew Nina was having lunch with Prince Nevsky and that Boris chap?'

'What Prince?' said Bernard. 'He's as dead as a dodo.'

'Well, why didn't she give the note to you?' asked Ashburner.

'I told you, mate. She was leaving when I got there. They both were. He was taking her to see Pasternak's grave. I wish to Christ I'd gone with them.'

'She was looking quite well, was she?' persisted Ashburner.

'As well as could be expected after seeing that bloody folk-art,' shouted Bernard, exasperated.

'I gather they were only tea-towels,' Ashburner said. 'Even so, I thought one or two of them were rather pretty.'

Enid, when she joined them, was wearing a black taffeta dress and carrying a dorothy bag made of threadbare velvet. When she sat down she rustled like falling tissue paper.

'Smashing texture,' enthused Bernard, and he stroked the surface of her bag as though it were a cat.

Ashburner, complimenting Enid insincerely on her smart appearance, considered her frock outmoded, to say the least; it was beginning to irritate him the way they all affected to admire anything old and second-hand no matter how appalling its condition. His wife had inherited an evening reticule embroidered with seed pearls from Uncle Robert's aunt. It was as good as new, strictly for show and insured for one hundred pounds. He was in the middle of telling them about it, describing the silver clasp, the flawlessness of its inner lining of ivory-coloured silk, when Bernard cried out belligerently, 'I'm warning you both, if the work exhibited this evening is of the same standard as that crap we were subjected to this afternoon, I'm walking out.'

Ashburner was both bewildered and offended. It was true that his wife sometimes acquired a far-away look in her eyes when he spoke to her for longer than a minute, but that was understandable, and though it would have been an exaggeration to pretend that his professional colleagues hung on his every word they would never had interrupted him in mid-sentence. It was part of his job to assess character and from what he had observed of Bernard over the last forty-eight hours it was difficult, despite his often boorish behaviour, to dismiss him as merely an ignorant fellow. There were depths of sensitivity in Bernard which, if the man had not been an

70

artist, Ashburner would have found disconcerting. There were only two rational explanations for his display of rudeness: either he was overtired from being up or down all night with Enid, or he was more worried than he cared to admit at the continuing absence of Nina.

Summoned by Olga Fiodorovna they left the restaurant and collected their coats from the cloakroom. Ashburner was astounded to see Bernard donning a Sherlock Holmes affair in expensive check tweed with a sort of cape attached to the shoulders. He couldn't understand how Bernard had managed to fit such a voluminous garment into a carrier bag. He was so markedly silent during the short drive to the People's Institute that Olga Fiodorovna linked her arm in his and begged him to cheer up.

'Tomorrow, Mr Douglas,' she promised, 'we shall find your suitcase. I give you my word.'

'Lovely,' he said and watching Bernard, who sat slumped in the front of the car, wondered if there was any significance in the dispirited droop of his head.

The lecture took place in a large room divided in half by a table and a row of metal chairs. Behind the table stood a dozen screens hung with drawings executed in very thin pencil. The audience faced the table. The English visitors sat self-consciously in front of the screens as though part of the exhibition. Throughout the lecture Olga Fiodorovna translated in an urgent whisper, loud enough to embarrass Ashburner but too low in pitch for him to hear distinctly. The phrase 'animal-lover' reached his ears, though he couldn't be sure of the context. He was on tenterhooks lest Bernard should erupt into anger; apart from having twisted round in his chair so that he now sat with his back to the audience, he appeared to be calmly studying those drawings closest to him. Once there was a commotion in the corridor outside and Ashburner looked up expectantly, heart racing, hoping as the door was flung open to see Nina sailing in, a ship come safe to port. He

71

was acutely disappointed when a powerfully built man, dressed as a factory worker in blue overalls and wearing a peaked cap like a harbour master, entered the room. In spite of his hat the fellow definitely wasn't a sissy, but there was something so luminous and compelling about his face that Ashburner found he was ogling him in much the same manner as he ogled Nina during those rare moments when she was nice to him. Closing the door boisterously behind him, the man sat down in the back row and tugged his cap over his eyes. Even with his face hidden he was obtrusive; arms spread wide he gripped the metal chairs on either side of him, as though otherwise he might hurtle through the body of the hall.

Now and then the lecturer addressed the English visitors directly. Enid regarded the speaker intently and with such an expression of anxiety that she gave the impression she was sitting beneath a tree that might fall on her. Every time she drew breath her taffeta frock crackled like a forest fire. Ashburner heard nothing. Listening to a foreign language, he thought, was similar to listening to classical music, which wasn't something he did often. If the sound was tuneful enough one noticed the first and last noises made by the orchestra; all the rest was drowned in day-dreams. As a youth with a boil on his neck he had gone once to a Promenade concert. The orchestra had played a particularly thunderous piece, and when the percussionist had stood up to clash his cymbals the boil had burst. Ashburner still bore the scar. Such faded blemishes were a tell-tale sign of a nineteen-forties adolescence, which was how he knew that Bernard was a post-war baby. Of course it was more difficult to tell with women because they had all that hair hanging down. He tried and failed to remember, except that her skin was a little too dark and her eyes somewhat too blue, the face of Nina. It was funny how women differed. His wife had been enormously fond of her uncle Robert, but she had never been back to Norwich since the funeral, not even to see the headstone, and yet Nina

72

was quite content to rush off in a blizzard to gawk at the grave of a perfect stranger. He wasn't sure how he should behave when he met her later in the evening. He would lose out if he attempted to be censorious or even if he capitulated and showed that he had missed her. He had missed – did miss – her dreadfully. There came to him the words of a song his wife was apt to sing, quaveringly, if the weather perked up. *I'll see you again, whenever spring breaks through again.* Startled, he clutched his pocket. Olga Fiodorovna jogged his elbow. Suddenly aware of applause he let go of Nina's scarf and clapped enthusiastically, head modestly inclined, for at that moment the lecturer was bowing to him.

Presently the audience stood and began to straggle between the chairs towards the upper end of the room. Olga Fiodorovna, sensing that Bernard was about to limp behind the screens, detained him. She laid hold of his arm and said, looking from him to the lecturer, 'Mr Chomsky is very glad to have you here. He apologises for the uncomfortable seating.'

Mr Chomsky nodded and smiled. Bernard stood like a sullen boy reprimanded unfairly for fighting in the playground. He refused to speak.

'Tell him,' said Ashburner, 'that we're glad to be here. We haven't yet had the opportunity to study his drawings, but we are sure they're excellent.'

'He is not the artist,' said Olga Fiodorovna. 'He is the Director of the Committee of the People's Institute and most interested to hear your views on English art at the present time.'

'Ah,' said Ashburner. He glanced nervously at Enid but she was fiddling with the belt of her frock. 'Tell him,' he said finally, 'that we do not pretend to be authorities on the subject.' He felt like Queen Victoria. Olga Fiodorovna frowned slightly and waited. She knew he was a coward.

'Tell him to get stuffed,' murmured Bernard.

At that instant a voice shouted 'Douglas.' Both Ashburner

and Bernard turned in response. They were each embraced by the man in the peaked cap.

Ashburner laughed heartily as he struggled to free himself. 'Who the devil is he?' he asked, when he had recovered his breath. The man was now hugging Enid; it sounded as if a parcel was being unwrapped and the paper torn into shreds.

'It's that mate of Nina's,' said Bernard. 'It's Boris.'

'Mr Shabelsky,' Olga Fiodorovna said. 'You are as tempestuous as ever.' She added a few words of Russian.

Boris smiled and shrugged his shoulders. 'Follow me,' he cried. 'You are going to have fun, I think', and seizing hold of Ashburner by the arm he ran him down the room.

Fearfully flustered, Ashburner collided with several chairs and, wincing, was half carried through the door.

In the street Boris invited Olga Fiodorovna to accompany them to the house of a friend. 'For supper,' he said. 'You are welcome.'

Olga disputed this. 'Besides,' she told him, 'I have the driver to consider. He is expecting to return Mr Douglas and the others to the hotel.'

'It was arranged yesterday with Karlovitch,' Boris said. 'You are talking arse-holes.'

'Where is Nina?' asked Ashburner. He had peered into the interiors of both the official car and the green vehicle which obviously belonged to Shabelsky. Olga took no notice of him. He overheard her telling the driver to go home.

'I'm hungry,' complained Enid. 'I'm terribly hungry.' She stood in the gutter in her swagger coat and allowed her teeth to chatter piteously. Boris opened the door of his car and she scuttled inside.

'Where is Nina?' repeated Ashburner. He took hold of Bernard.

Shaking him off, Bernard clambered into the back seat beside the rustling Enid.

'Mr Shabelsky,' said Olga Fiodorovna. 'The driver refuses

to wait. He is going home. I am forced to ask you to run me to my apartment.'

Ashburner stayed stubbornly on the pavement. He hadn't shaved that morning and under the light of the street lamp he looked dissolute and unkempt. He was clutching Nina's pink scarf to his chest.

'Will you look at him,' shouted Boris. 'What a brigand the man is.' Opening the rear door he bundled Ashburner into the car.

11

Boris's friend was a handsome woman with dyed red hair who lived with her elderly husband in the middle of a forest fifty kilometres from Moscow. Her name was Tatiana and she was a painter. Though her guests failed to arrive until after midnight she was delighted to see them. With her own hands she bathed Ashburner's wound and applied a square of sticking plaster to his nose.

For some of the long journey into the dark countryside Ashburner had been under the mistaken impression that they were on their way to pick up Nina from the Peking Hotel. He had thought they were taking a roundabout route because first they had delivered Olga Fiodorovna to her Mamotchka. After a further hour's driving, realising he had been misled and in spite of the tremendous din inside the car, he had fallen into a stupor compounded of misery and exhaustion. Boris Shabelsky had sung many songs, all of them loudly, discussed art furiously with Bernard and conducted a rowdy flirtation with Enid. Forty kilometres outside Moscow, brandishing his fist in the air, he had recited most of the Charge of the Light Brigade. Sometimes for what seemed like minutes he took both hands off the wheel.

The car had finally stopped in a narrow lane banked by snow in the heart of a forest. Before the headlamps were extinguished a low building with a wooden veranda had been identified in the distance; a red lantern swung above the

76

porch. The vicious barking of dogs blared through the trees. Boris had instructed them to get out of the car slowly and, ignoring the dogs, to walk calmly and boldly along the path to the *dacha*. One dog, he warned, was as big as a wolf and the other was tiny and called Betty. Of the two, Betty was the more dangerous animal. 'If you are attacked,' he had advised, 'Lash out. Do not bother to be British.'

Stumbling from the car, Ashburner had been given little opportunity to display either his calmness or his boldness. Almost immediately the larger dog had leapt upon him. It hadn't bitten him, but its head struck the bridge of his nose with such force that he cried out. He had thought he'd outpaced Betty, but as he ran she overtook him. Booted by Bernard, she flew through the air and bounced squealing from a snow-covered bush. Ashburner had time to observe, before he ran headlong up the steps and into the *dacha*, that she appeared to have only three legs. Someone on a previous occasion, he presumed, had sensibly kicked off the fourth.

Once the slight cut on his nose had been attended to, he was led into the living room where a log fire burned in the open hearth. 'How lovely,' he said, and would have stared mesmerised into the flames if Boris Shabelsky hadn't engaged him in conversation. He wanted to know Ashburner's opinion of Russia.

'Well,' said Ashburner, 'we're mostly sitting inside cars. And then, of course, everything is covered in snow.'

'You've been to Red Square,' Boris said. 'They always take you to Red Square.' In spite of his factory worker's clothing he stood in front of the fire in the swaggering attitude of a lion tamer. He hadn't yet removed his cap. 'You saw Lenin's tomb, I suppose. It is very historical, don't you agree?'

'From the outside,' said Ashburner. He wasn't sure what history was, beyond a sense of place; he would remember the Square, with or without its mausoleum, because there he had witnessed Bernard over-run by the Red Army.

He was just about to ask Boris where Pasternak's grave was situated and how Nina had managed to appreciate it in the dark, when he was directed to sit beside Tatiana's elderly husband on a wooden bench wedged between the table and the wall. A glass vase filled with yellow tulips stood in the centre of the cloth amid a feast. Believing that the numerous dishes of caviar and quails' eggs and pickled fish comprised the whole of the meal, the English visitors tackled everything spread before them. Five bottles of Georgian wine were opened and emptied and more bottles fetched from the kitchen.

The heat in the room was intense. Beyond the shuttered windows the dogs still bayed. Ashburner's enjoyment of his food was marred by the ramblings of the elderly husband who spoke only Russian but, through his wife and Boris, insisted on telling him a confusing anecdote involving ikons and churches. Ashburner found it frightfully tiring listening to him; even when translated into English he didn't understand the point of the story. He felt that he and the old man were being treated like children, thrown scraps of information merely to keep them quiet. He didn't mind being out of the mainstream of the conversation. None of them had the faintest idea of small talk and they weren't listening to one another. He thought Bernard was behaving like a ruffian, slopping wine all over the cloth and not caring where he put his egg shells. 'What bugger,' he was demanding, flushed with drink and thumping the table, 'imagined that exhibition had anything to do with Art?'

'I have seen shows as bad in London,' defended Boris. 'Some worse. You have your establishment artists. We have ours. What is the difference?'

'He is very troubled,' said Tatiana, speaking to Ashburner. 'He would like your opinion on the matter. He went with a friend, a friend from England, to a church outside Moscow –'

'You're not allowed to paint what you want,' cried Bernard.

78

'You've thrown private patronage out of the window and given it all to the State. That's the difference.'

'But the private patrons equally told the artist what to do,' protested Boris. He turned to Ashburner. 'I am an old man. I like to give pleasure. My friend is keen on ikons.'

'All those portraits,' shouted Tatiana. 'All those religious subjects, those narrative paintings –'

'You're not allowed to do what you want to do,' said Enid. She jabbed Bernard's arm with her fork. 'Not really. You can do it, but it doesn't follow anyone will give you a show. Look what happened with your rabbit etchings. All they want you for is to drop bricks on the telly.'

'He has known this friend for many years,' translated Tatiana. 'They understand one another. That is why it is difficult to refuse him the ikons. I have not heard of the rabbits, only the series of girls with ducks –'

'Geese,' corrected Bernard. 'And anyway they were shown –'

'But not at Delbanco's,' said Enid. 'And you didn't sell any.'

'They are very old, very beautiful, maybe four hundred years old,' Tatiana said. She rose from the table and went into the kitchen. She called out: 'Not many people come to look, and his friend is mad for them. So in the end it is arranged and his friend takes them.' She came back into the living room carrying a dish of roasted pheasants. 'So what would you advise?' She looked searchingly at Ashburner.

'Good gracious,' exclaimed Ashburner. 'Is there more to eat?'

'You're supposed to have cracked it,' complained Bernard. 'You get rent-free studios, subsidised tickets to the Bolshoi, *dachas* in the bloody country –'

'Defect, my friend,' shouted Boris, and he bellowed with laughter and struck Bernard repeatedly on the shoulder.

The mystery of the ikons was never satisfactorily explained.

79

Ashburner couldn't think why the Englishman hadn't been arrested going through customs. He wasn't altogether sure what an ikon was, but it sounded a rather spikey sort of object to smuggle successfully out of the country. Perhaps the Englishman had been caught and the old man was appealing to him for help.

'Are you all right?' asked Enid. She leaned across the table at him, holding a portion of pheasant in her fingers.

Ashburner confessed he felt a little warm. He glanced enviously at Bernard, who had removed his corduroy jacket and sat with sleeves rolled up to the elbow.

'Has he met Boris before?' he asked. 'They seem very thick.'

'No,' said Enid. 'Bernard's like that with everyone, providing he likes them. He's marvellous, isn't he?'

'He's on pills, you know,' said Ashburner. 'I suppose they're pain-killers, are they? For his hip?'

But Enid wasn't listening to him. She was gazing at Bernard as though he were the Archangel Gabriel.

Ashburner wondered if Nina would be able to manage without the pills that were in his missing suitcase. It was thoughtful, if unfortunate, the way she had entrusted them to him – thoughtful but odd, because she could just as easily have slipped them into her handbag. Surely she hadn't brought enteritis tablets to a cold country? There couldn't be anything wrong with the water supply, though it was true everyone seemed to prefer vodka.

Several times he tried to ask Boris when he had last seen Nina, but he was always ignored. Bernard and he were drunkenly discussing politics and religion. Religious fervour freed man from the necessity to live each day as though it were the last. The good times lay beyond the grave. In the words of someone – Ashburner didn't think they could be Bernard's – 'Was it not a sweet thing to have all covetousness satisfied, suspicion and infidelity removed, courage and joy infused?' Purification of the heart in the religious and Catholic sense was to be obtained by constant docility in the leadings of the Holy Ghost. For the believer, Communism offered an equally angelic solution to living. All that was required was an allegiance to the Perfect State.

'Tommy rot,' cried Ashburner, maddened by their indifference to him. But the very words, *sweet thing* and *infidelity removed*, touched him to the core. Rendered almost unconscious by the quantities of wine he had drunk, he rested his head on the table, his cheek lying in the bloody debris of a pomegranate, and groaned aloud.

Tatiana assisted him from the bench and sat him down on the leather sofa in front of the dying fire. She hugged him. The warmth of her embrace and the sight of those glowing embers glimpsed beyond the circle of her arms brought tears to his eyes.

When eventually he could speak he apologised for his emotional behaviour. 'You've been terribly hospitable,' he said. 'The pheasant was delicious, and I did find Mr Tatiana's story most amusing. Normally I would have been more on the ball.'

He was horrified to hear himself whimpering. He tugged at the plaster on his nose and attempted to sit upright, but his hostess held him fast. He confided to her the pathetic history of the elusive Nina, his lost suitcase, his unworkable shower.

'No one answers me,' he concluded. 'Whenever I ask where she is, I'm fobbed off. I'm only here because I'm supposed to be her companion. Why else should I be lolloping about the Soviet Union?'

'My dear man,' soothed Tatiana. 'She is at the hotel. On the way to Pasternak's grave she felt unwell and Boris took her back.' Releasing him, she waved her arm to attract the attention of Boris. 'Tell him what happened at Petrov's studio. The poor man is distressed.'

'She noticed the floor,' Boris shouted. 'You know how it is with Nina. Petrov didn't want to tell her but she was

81

stubborn. She thrives on such things. Later, she felt sick.'

'What am I to make of that?' asked Ashburner irritably. He fumbled in his pocket for Nina's note. 'Read that,' he said, pushing the scrap of paper into Tatiana's hand. 'I think you'll find it pretty straightforward.'

Tatiana looked at him curiously. 'Don't you get it?' demanded Ashburner. 'The last line should read, "See you when *I* get back." After all, she's the one that keeps disappearing, not me.'

'Calm yourself,' murmured Tatiana. 'You will feel better after a nice hot bath.' Uttering sugary little cries of reassurance, she levered him up off the sofa and took him into the bathroom. She turned on the taps and fetched him a clean shirt belonging to her husband. She begged him not to close the door. 'There is something wrong with the catch,' she explained. 'No one will play the voyeur.'

Removing his clothes, Ashburner thrust the door shut and climbing into the bath fell blissfully asleep. He had a frightening dream in which he was Noah trying to shepherd the animals into the Ark. He had to wrestle with a kangaroo who was trying to stamp a goose to death. In the distance he could see Nina in a rowing boat and he knew she was trying to reach him, but the gap between Ark and boat was widening, not diminishing. He woke, shivering in cool water. Towelling himself dry, he put on the borrowed shirt and, fully dressed, attempted to leave the bathroom. The door wouldn't budge. He hammered on it for several minutes, but nobody came. Recollecting that he was on the ground floor, he opened the window and clambered on to the sill; barking hideously, the wolf dog hurtled from the shadows of the veranda.

12

The next morning, the instant he woke, Ashburner recalled in detail the events of the night. Far from inhibiting him, the remembrance of such ludicrous events afforded him a sense of release. It was as though previously he had been trapped within a monstrous butterfly net; in some miraculous fashion he now regained his freedom. He leapt from his bed without the trace of a headache. Filled with resolve, he sought out Bernard in the breakfast bar on the third floor of the hotel, and pausing only to order a bowl of yoghourt and a pannikin of fried eggs outlined what had to be done.

'That Fedora girl,' he said, 'will have to get hold of another key and gain an entrance. We've been far too remiss as it is.'

Bernard found it difficult not to stare at his companion. The plaster on Ashburner's nose had turned black at the edges, and there was a large rent in the sleeve of his jacket. 'You're quite sure,' he asked, 'that there's no reply from her room?'

'I didn't say that,' reprimanded Ashburner. 'A man answered. Naturally I didn't understand what he said, but he was obviously annoyed. The whole thing is peculiar. That Boris chap for instance, a perfect stranger, ordering us to go to an exhibition and then taking us out for supper.'

'People are always taking me out for supper,' Bernard said. 'Most of them are strange.'

'We never even got a peep at the drawings,' countered Ashburner, whose own social engagements were usually strictly supervised by his wife. 'And anyway, nobody's yet explained who he is. And what about Nina being sick on the studio floor? I don't like the sound of it.'

Bernard thought Ashburner had led a sheltered life, or else he had more imagination than would be expected. 'You're making too much of it,' he said, and waited until Ashburner had eaten his eggs. 'Look, mate,' he began. 'I shouldn't worry about Nina being off-colour. She's not actually ill, you know. There's an explanation.'

Ashburner felt as though he had been punched in the stomach. 'Do you mean it's her time of the month?' he asked. It was terrible to think that Bernard knew her so intimately.

'How the hell should I know,' said Bernard. 'I just meant that she's not really ill.'

They discussed the situation with Enid while they waited in the lobby for Olga Fiodorovna. Enid yawned repeatedly and sagged against a pillar. She couldn't be absolutely sure that Ashburner wasn't making a mountain out of a mole-hill.

'You seem to forget,' he protested, 'that we haven't set eyes on her for thirty-six hours.'

'Some of those were in the night,' she argued. 'Besides, Bernard saw her yesterday afternoon.'

Bernard admitted that this was inaccurate. A car had driven away as he had arrived at the illustrator's studio and someone had waved at him. He had assumed it was Nina. 'At least,' he said, 'Karlovitch told me that she had just left in a car.'

'There you are,' cried Ashburner triumphantly, and he paced conspicuously about the lobby in his torn jacket.

When Olga Fiodorovna came, she took the wind out of his sails. Before he could utter a word she announced that Mrs St Clair had been taken ill in the night and had been removed to a sanatorium.

'A sanatorium?' he cried. 'Was that necessary?' He could only think of tuberculosis. Even Bernard looked shaken.

'Do you think we have kidnapped your friend?' Olga Fiodorovna asked crossly. 'It is a rest home for painters and writers. Here in Russia it is quite normal for creative artists to be treated with respect. Mrs St Clair is evidently over-tired. You can telephone her later. In a day or two she will travel to Leningrad and join us.'

A curious but happy incident took place before they were taken to have lunch with the committee of the Artists' Union. While Olga Fiodorovna was away pursuing her paperwork, they were again deposited in the English bar of the Hotel Nationale. On her way from the Ladies' room Enid noticed a British Airways sign in the corridor. Without consulting the others she went up to the seventh floor and entered the offices of the airline. There were two men seated in armchairs and a young woman behind a desk. Enid said she was inquiring on behalf of a friend of hers who had lost his luggage three days ago. She didn't give a name.

The man seated nearest to the door immediately stood up and said in English, 'It is at the airport. It's been waiting since yesterday.'

Startled, Enid expressed her joy and surprise, though as she later told Ashburner she could have been knocked down with a feather. It was a mystery how the man knew to which suitcase she was referring. He telephoned the airport in her presence, gave Ashburner's correct name, nodded his head and putting down the phone confirmed that she could collect the baggage any time she wished. The second man, who was wearing horn-rimmed spectacles, didn't say anything. Only when running excitedly down the corridor did she realise that she had seen him on another occasion; he was the aeroplane passenger who had been so preoccupied with his briefcase.

Ashburner, delighted at the news, insisted they abandon their coffee drinking in favour of something stronger. He didn't care why or how the man on the seventh floor had known about his luggage. 'Everything here,' he said, 'is

85

cloaked in intrigue. I don't give a hoot as long as I have a change of underclothing.'

He and Enid talked about whether it would be a courteous gesture to buy Tatiana's husband a new shirt to replace the torn one. It would certainly be courteous, Enid said, but why on earth should he? After all, it had been their animal who had nearly ripped off his arm when he fell out of the bathroom window. And she didn't suppose they were thinking of replacing his jacket.

'Will you both come with me?' Ashburner asked. 'To that studio by the lake. There's something bothering me about he place.'

Enid agreed, but Bernard said wild horses wouldn't drag him back.

When Olga Fiodorovna returned, even before she had time to sit down, Enid cried out: 'The suitcase – it's been found.'

'I regret not,' said Olga Fiodorovna. 'But we are doing our best.' Having heard the whole story and the fact that at this moment the suitcase was waiting to be picked up from the airport, she gave the impression that they had been talking at cross purposes. Of course she was aware that the suitcase had been run to ground; she meant that as yet no one had gone to collect it. She urged them to finish their drinks, because otherwise they would be late for their next appointment.

'Would it be convenient,' asked Ashburner, 'to return to that fellow's studio in the suburbs? I was enormously impressed by his illustrations and I don't think I did them justice. I suppose I was thinking more about seeing Nina.'

'It will not be convenient,' Olga Fiodorovna said. 'Your luncheon with the Artists' Union will go on for hours, and you must remember we are taking the night train to Leningrad.'

'I see,' said Ashburner. 'Well, could I please have the telephone number of that Boris character? We would like to thank him for his kindness.'

Olga intimated that it was part of Mr Shabelsky's job to be

kind to foreigners. There was no need to thank him. Unless they hurried they would be late for lunch.

'There is every need,' Ashburner said. He was careful not to look at her. 'And I don't think I can go anywhere until I have spoken to him.'

It took Olga Fiodorovna almost three-quarters of an hour to contact Boris Shabelsky. In the interim Ashburner ordered more drinks, ate a quantity of peanuts and refrained from apologising to anyone. When he was finally summoned into the corridor of the hotel he thanked the interpreter politely, and making no attempt to pick up the receiver waited until she had reluctantly walked away from him into the bar.

The luncheon given in honour of the English artists and held at the one time home of Prince Nevsky began as a formal affair. They ate at a long table set beneath the overhang of a massive oak staircase which led up to a gallery hung with paintings. It was impossible for Ashburner to grasp with whom he was lunching. Remembering, let alone pronouncing, the names of the numerous persons introduced to him was out of the question. One face was very like another; only the two women stood out. Enid's breasts rested on the cloth and sprigs of parsley spiked her blouse; round-shouldered from lack of sleep she slumped against the edge of the table. No sooner had the company sat down than they were on their feet, bidden by Mr Karlovitch to drink a toast of friendship to artists the world over, and more especially those of the Soviet Union and Britain. 'To a true and frank exchange of ideas,' he cried optimistically, and raised his glass. Much to Ashburner's relief, once this token reference had been made the subject of Art was never again mentioned. He was seated between a youngish man dressed like a stockbroker and a bespectacled person who, constantly seized by surprise, pursed his lips from time to time and audibly whistled two or three notes on a rising scale. He and most of his fellow committee-members spoke English or American and had visited London on several

87

occasions during the past few years.

After a quarter of an hour of laboured conversation it became evident that a true and frank exchange would not be achieved. No one had any ideas worth exchanging. They're just like us, thought Ashburner, neither better nor worse; he had attended many lunches in the City with people he didn't know, simply for the sake of business. He gathered there were few actual artists in the room. A General was pointed out to him and an Admiral, both retired. He supposed they were Sunday painters, rather like Churchill and Roosevelt. The real painters, he imagined, if they were anything like Boris Shabelsky and his friend Tatiana, were all in homes for the alcoholic.

Quite soon he became involved in a harangue on property values in London and the rise in the cost of living in relation to workers' wages. The people he addressed didn't seem particularly interested in his views, and to his astonishment he suspected that he had instigated the discussion in the first place; far from defending beliefs he had held for a lifetime, he realised he was actually implying that the system was unjust and the investing of money immoral. He went further and indicated that educational standards in England, both in the private and the state sector, had collapsed, that consumer madness was rotting the fibre of the people and that a fairer distribution of wealth was vital. He couldn't think what had got into him. He had never been known to vote Labour, his wife and he owned shares in Burmah Oil, and at the drop of a hat he was always more than ready to criticise the car workers at Dagenham. This is all due to my upbringing, he reasoned. If I am not careful, excessive politeness will have me warbling the Red Flag. Moments later, hearing a man telling Bernard that his wife kept a servant, and hardly able to believe his ears, he cried out 'A servant, a *servant*?' in tones of such critical severity that Bernard leaned across the table and ordered him to belt up. 'You're overdoing the flat cap and brown boots number, mate,' he hissed.

There was talk of the Café Royal, the House of Lords, the London Palladium and other places of interest. Ashburner hadn't been to any of them and he had never even heard of the Round House in Chalk Farm. The food at the Café Royal was apparently excellent, but when two of Russia's most distinguished ballet dancers had appeared at the Palladium right-wing agitators had thrown tintacks on to the stage. Ashburner, who had never got the hang of ballet, found this amusing and smiled broadly. Though he was still anxious about Nina, it was difficult for him to remain gloomy in the midst of such cordiality and warmth. He became expert, whenever a toast was proposed, at leaping to his feet and swallowing his measure of vodka at one gulp.

Mr Karlovitch confided that it was always a problem when in London to choose a suitable present to bring home to his young son. 'Though,' he said, 'I am happy shopping for clothes in Bond Street. The material and cut are splendid.'

'Next time you're in London,' advised Ashburner, 'give me a tinkle and I'll take you to my Oxfam shop. I always go there for my sports jackets. As for the child, there's a little shop I know just off the Kings Road. Micky Mouse tee shirts, pop records, outspoken badges – that sort of thing.'

'My son,' Mr Karlovitch said, 'is very scientific, very technically minded. He is interested in computers.'

Ashburner dropped the subject. His own sons, both over twenty-one and expensively educated, couldn't be said to be interested in anything, certainly not in anything as advanced as computers.

To facilitate the burgeoning of new conversations, everybody swopped places in the middle of the meal – everyone except Bernard, who wouldn't budge on account of his leg, and Mr Karlovitch who, blatantly cheating, jumped three spaces in order to sit beside Enid. The man given to whistling now sat at the right hand side of Olga Fiodorovna and opposite Ashburner. The interpreter said little; often she consulted her wristwatch and frowned.

Someone asked Ashburner if he was enjoying his visit. Was the Soviet Union all he had expected? Had it proved to be an eye-opener? Ashburner admitted that so far he had had very little sleep. 'But,' he added, 'speaking for myself, I am enjoying it enormously.' He was telling no more than the truth. His suitcase had been located and the mystery of Nina's constant disappearances temporarily solved. He had stopped swimming against the tide. If the airport authorities had been in touch with his wife, then all was up with him. There was no point in rushing home to be assassinated. If they hadn't, he might as well stay. It would require a mountain of paper and a special dispensation from the Kremlin to be sent back early to England; he had reached the point of no return. He couldn't help noticing that Mr Karlovitch had his arm about Enid's waist. She was on about the Polar Trek North. Ashburner wouldn't have thought her the loose type, or Karlovitch for that matter, though these days that sort of thing was rife in every camp.

'Captain Scott in his tent', Enid was saying, 'was far more concerned with pleasing his wife than conquering the Pole.'

Ashburner found this incredible. He hadn't know that Mrs Scott had gone on the expedition. When he thought of how his own wife complained of draughts in the sitting room, he felt ashamed for her. Nina, as far as he could judge, wasn't namby-pamby about home comforts. She had once told him she had sat up for three nights on a train to Istanbul. She wasn't the sort to witness a street accident and faint. When she had been knocked from her bicycle as a child, she swore she hadn't cried. Boris Shabelsky was wrong in thinking that the brutal account of sudden death in Petrov's studio had made her sick. When I telephone her tonight, he thought, I shan't hide my true feelings. It will need courage, but there is a way of getting through to her. He would, he told himself, have liked to know more about the country he was in, the politics, the man at the top, but he

90

already understood that this was impossible. The man at the top, rumoured in the Western press to be dying, was merely a figurehead. One could sing for ever *Come out, come out, wherever you are*, and no one would answer. It was an idea that governed, not a person. 'Did you know?' he asked Olga Fiodorovna, 'that when Colonel Fawcett went into the jungles of Bolivia, a particularly revolting form of river parasite abounded? It burrowed into the body and laid its eggs under the skin.'

Olga Fiodorovna raised her eyebrows; her companion whistled.

'You've got it in one,' shouted Ashburner. 'Only way to catch sight of the buggers. A little whistle, out pops the grub, and Bob's your uncle.'

At that instant the man dressed as a stockbroker stood up. The voices died away. Bernard, swearing atrociously, was the last to become silent.

'I would like,' the stockbroker said, 'for us to remember our absent guest. We have each of us known her. And to know her, in the words of your English poet, is to love her. Gentlemen and ladies, let us drink to the rapid recovery of our dear friend, Mrs St Clair.'

The company struggled to its feet, some swaying, some holding on to one another for support. 'Mrs St Clair,' they chorused.

'What does it mean?' asked Ashburner of Enid. 'How do they know her?'

'Hush,' said Enid, for the stockbroker was now taking a piece of paper from his pocket and unfolding it. 'I will read this in Russian,' he said. 'Our interpreter will translate to you its original flavour.' He commenced to recite what appeared to be a poem.

Ashburner hadn't cared for the wording of the toast. It had been altogether too familiar. He wanted to make some protest, like sitting down, but he wasn't sure if he was in the right and even if he had been he wasn't brave enough to show active displeasure. Inwardly he growled like a tiger.

When the stockbroker had finished declaiming, there was laughter and applause.

'I can't stand poetry,' grumbled Bernard. 'It's usually bloody rubbish.'

'This is a work,' announced Olga Fiodorovna, studying the scrap of exercise paper handed to her, 'dedicated to Mrs St Clair. It begins, *Nina, Nina, your window is always open.* Then there is a pause. It goes on, *Oft have I waited in the hours that are small, waited for the light that will shine through the trees. Drawn through the darkness to that port of call in Holland Park –*'

'My God,' exclaimed Ashburner. 'She has a studio there.'

'*I have not been disappointed,*' continued Olga Fiodorovna. '*I have not been let down. The heart's warmth, like a candle flame, is not easily extinguished. For Nina, Nina, your window is always open.*'

'See what I mean?' said Bernard. 'Candle flames go out all the bloody time.'

There were several more verses, but Ashburner didn't hear them. There was no doubt in his mind that the stanzas so merrily received were totally suspect. What was being read aloud bore more relation to a rendering of Eskimo Nell than to an ode to a visiting dignitary. If I telephone her later, he thought, I will guard my true feelings. I mustn't make an ass of myself.

When the luncheon was over, Enid, who earlier had expressed a wish to look more closely at a painting of Lenin inciting some shipyard workers to rebellion, was seen climbing the Gothic staircase to the gallery, supported by Mr Karlovitch. Olga Fiodorovna followed discreetly.

Ashburner and Bernard, without warning, were driven off in the official car to a palace to take tea with a metal worker. The glass dome in the banqueting hall that now served as a workshop had cracked under the weight of successive winter snows and the mouldings above the doors were stained with

92

damp. Within minutes of arrival Bernard fell deeply asleep while studying a portfolio of preliminary drawings. Ashburner was obliged to enthuse, single-handed, over a series of raised reliefs of naked women with rippling hair. Later he was subjected to a demonstration of the artist's skill. The metal worker, unable to speak English, performed his task in silence save for the muted blows of his hammer. Perched on a rickety stool Ashburner gazed intently at the surface of the work bench shimmering under a layer of zinc and copper filings, and reflected on the curious fate of the previous occupant of the studio beside the frozen lake. Unknown assailants had entered the premises in daylight and surprising the artist, a specialist in humorous cartoons, at his desk had clubbed him to death. Nothing had been stolen. Boris Shabelsky had vehemently denied the existence of hooliganism in the Soviet Union. It had been a *crime passionnel*. Ashburner was uncertain why he himself should feel so shocked by an incident that had become commonplace in England. He was after all used to eating his breakfast, without loss of appetite, to the accompaniment of that breezy voice on the radio listing arson and mugging and rape. He thought that perhaps his feeling of unease was due in part to Bernard's dissertation on their first night in Moscow when, in response to a facetious remark of Enid's regarding the poor quality of the service in the restaurant, he had referred to Mother Russia as a 'concept above and beyond their experience'. They were visiting the first country to embrace Communism; sympathy or disagreement with the political theory was unimportant. The myth, right or wrong, had become reality. According to Bernard it was as if they were visiting a country in which the teachings of Jesus had been put into practice. He insisted he was the last person to have any truck with either Bolshevism or Christianity, but there was no denying the fact of the 'reality'. At which point Ashburner had lost track of the argument – in any case he was too busy wondering whether or

93

not Nina would allow him to her room – but it had something to do with bread queues and Enid having been rung up by the Press last year and asked how many pairs of knickers she owned, simply because the Tate Gallery had purchased one of her paintings. The discussion had continued at the home of Boris's friend Tatiana, but there again Ashburner had been preoccupied, this time with the elderly husband, though he had heard Boris explaining that queues were caused because bread and other such things were subsidised by the State. Boris had also admitted that as an artist, and therefore a privileged and respected member of society, he had never had to queue for anything. Nor was it likely that *Pravda* would dream of enquiring about the number or colour of his underpants. The exact meaning behind this discourse had eluded Ashburner, but the general idea remained with him like a fishbone in the gullet. *The murder of an artist was an attack on the State.* Startled, he rocked on his stool. He realised that until this moment he had never been stimulated by abstract thought. He had always known, even before Nina put it into words, that his schooldays had crippled his development. Equally he had always understood that his strength of character, his honesty, the stability of his marriage and his acceptance of responsibility were a direct result of this emotional damage. In his case, the ends had more than justified the means. If the world hadn't changed so drastically in the nineteen-sixties – he dated the onset of the permissive society as preceding the Profumo Affair and following the case of the Duchess of Argyll – he would never in the nineteen-seventies have gone off the rails. Unlike Nina, whose window was always open, he had been content with his enclosed existence. His involvement with her, furtive and inconclusive in the sense that he could never protect her, father her children, foot the bill for her private dental treatment, had left his attitude to life unaltered. She had bothered him, frustrated him in much the same fashion as his wife continued to bother

94

and frustrate him, but he hadn't been shaken to the core. Now, alone in a foreign country and inexplicably functioning more or less normally without the support of either wife or mistress – he hadn't even missed his dog – he began dimly to rediscover that lost boy who, compelled at school to read certain set novels of Dostoyevsky, had for a brief twelve months feebly wrestled with the notion of divine justice and self-punishment. Can it be, he thought, smiling and nodding appreciatively at the metal worker, that Mother Russia is a catalyst?

At midnight, reunited with his suitcase, he was the most alert member of the small party that wearily boarded the night express to Leningrad.

13

In the morning, travelling from station to hotel, no one spoke. Olga Fiodorovna was too tired to deliver an historical lecture on the architectural splendours of the city. The hired car bounced over numerous bridges above canals edged with ancient houses washed in pastel shades of blue and pink. They drove through falling snow along cobbled streets and passed in silence the monumental columns of malachite and lapis lazuli that fronted St Isaac's Cathedral. When the car halted, blocked by a barricade of thrown-up earth and concrete mixers, it was some moments before the interpreter realised that they had stopped. The ground in front of the Hotel Metropole was being dug up by lady roadmenders. A woman in a crash helmet of acid yellow, grey hair netted in snowflakes and hanging limply to the shoulders of her quilted jacket, was maneuvering a bulldozer backwards and forwards in the ruined street.

Mr Karlovitch suggested they should get out and walk the few remaining yards. Olga Fiodorovna wouldn't hear of it; defying the raised fists and warning flags of the construction workers, she goaded the driver to mount the embankment of rubble. Lurching down the far side and dipping under the maw of the dirt-shifter, which at that very moment was lowering to grab and pulverise, the car rocked and juddered over the potholes to the smashed kerb at the entrance of the hotel.

The Metropole, smaller than the Peking and more luxurious, provided Ashburner with a hot bath. No matter that the water gushing from the hot taps was a brackish brown. There was even a bath plug. Refreshed, he opened his suitcase and found its contents in disarray. One of his waders was missing. The tops had gone both from his tube of shaving cream and from his Colgate toothpaste. The turn-ups of his old tweed trousers had been interfered with and the pockets pulled inside out.

He wished he had time to sit quietly in a corner and think everything over, but Olga Fiodorovna had said they must be downstairs in the lobby by nine-thirty sharp. They were going to the Hermitage to look closely at the Impressionists. The business of the suitcase is puzzling, he thought, adjusting his tie with hands that trembled from fatigue, but can't be compared with the perplexing events on the midnight express. He had begun by sharing a sleeping compartment with Mr Karlovitch. The women occupied the one next door. Bernard had been installed in a single-berth cabin at the end of the corridor; after only a few moments he had reappeared, complaining that he couldn't settle until the train had actually started. The men had remained fully clothed and upright, enjoying two bottles of wine provided by the Committee of the Artists' Union. Presently Enid had emerged from her compartment barefooted and wearing a long white nightgown beneath something she referred to as a 'happy' coat. They had asked her to sit with them, but she was worried lest a ticket collector or guard should take exception to her state of undress. Instead she had loitered exotically in the doorway, drinking out of a paper cup – the voluminous sleeve of her coat, embroidered with gold and scarlet thread, falling back to expose an arm flecked to the elbow with green paint. Now and then she had exchanged glances with the Secretary of the Union. When an hour or so had passed and the train was at last clanking slowly through the suburbs of Moscow, Mr

97

Karlovitch had asked Bernard if he would mind changing compartments with him. 'I am a sickly sleeper,' he had told him. 'The least noise and I am jumping up. I am afraid I will disturb the good Mr Douglas.'

'I don't care where I doss down,' Bernard had said. 'I can sleep on the edge of a cliff.'

There had been some horseplay with Ashburner's fishing rod. Bernard had mentioned that its canvas cylinder was the ideal container for transporting drawings. He had insisted on fitting the rod together so that it buckled against the roof. After wrestling with Bernard for possession of his rod, Ashburner had gone to the lavatory and then for a stroll along the corridors. In his estimation the view from the windows had been much the same as from any train going through the outskirts of any city in the small hours; a few fitful lights, a stretch of darkness, the green and livid glow of an industrial complex working through the night. He had pressed his cheek to the cold glass – the heat inside the train was oppressive – and had felt for a brief moment a sense of loneliness or adventure, which in his case he thought was probably the same thing. On his return he had found both men lying on their respective bunks, fully clothed and inert. Mr Karlovitch was clutching an empty bottle of wine to his chest and had evidently been guilty of exaggeration. Shaken quite roughly, he hadn't stirred. Switching off the meagre light, Ashburner had made his way to the single berth cabin.

At first he had been unable to sleep. Earlier in the evening, when he had reminded Olga Fiodorovna of her promise that he should speak to Nina at the sanatorium, she had fobbed him off with a preposterous story of peak-hour telephones and unobtainable numbers. He hadn't been in a fit state to argue with her. He was childishly deflected at the sight of his suitcase in the lobby, and neither Bernard nor Enid had backed him up. The moment had passed and he had realised he would have to wait the four hundred miles until they arrived in Leningrad. Lying on his bunk he had thought he couldn't wait and he did remember worrying about his lack of backbone. Then, he supposed, he had dropped asleep, because the next minute he was dreaming he had fallen out of a hammock; he could see the black strings trembling and criss-crossing above his head. At the same time he had become aware that his wife was caressing him in a violent manner. In his dream he had rolled on top of her, penetrated her, and it had all been over in the flick of a cow's tail. He imagined it had something to do with the motion of the train on the track. He had only known he was awake when he distinctly heard the door sliding shut and found himself lying on the floor of the compartment with his vest rolled up to his navel. For at least three hours after the incident he had knelt on his bunk, staring out at the flying night.

He could be forgiven for thinking the whole matter had been a dream. In twenty-three years his wife hadn't made the slightest attempt to arouse him, not since returning from that New Year's Eve party at the Hammerskills when she had accused him of lasciviously eyeing Marjorie Hammerskill. Stung by the injustice of her insinuation, he hadn't a thought in his head but to get his own little wife between the sheets – seeing that he paid for the food she ate and the clothes she wore – he had slapped her cruelly across the face. Before the cry of remorse had left his lips she had responded in a manner both wanton and surprising. He tried slapping her again, a month later, but on that occasion the result had been her refusal to speak to him for several weeks.

He still had no idea of the identity of the woman who had so abruptly seduced him. Was it Olga Fiodorovna or Enid? He wasn't prudish, but he did like to know with whom he was being intimate – and then again a man preferred to do some of the running. It was in his nature. It wasn't as if he was a nocturnal animal, doomed like a hamster to couple in darkness. To be accurate, he realised he hadn't often coupled in daylight – beyond a few countable summer evenings before the children were born and those unsatisfactory noon-times spent with Nina.

When he went downstairs he found the others assembled at the booking desk. He apologised for keeping them waiting. 'Someone's been messing about with my case,' he said. 'They've taken one of my wellies.'

'You haven't kept us waiting,' said Bernard. 'Olga doesn't like her room.'

'I love beauty,' explained Olga Fiodorovna. 'I cannot bear the commonplace. I will not sleep a wink unless my room is well proportioned and furnished with taste.' She had changed into an elegant black trouser suit and was wearing ankle boots of scarlet leather.

'About phoning Nina,' began Ashburner, but already she had turned away from him.

Enid told Ashburner he looked dreadful. 'You've got great black circles under your eyes,' she said.

He didn't think she was hinting at anything. She wasn't winking at him or leaning against him in a familiar manner. 'I'm all right, my dear,' he said. 'It's just that I'm not yet in my stride.'

He was convinced it hadn't been Enid who had come to his compartment. She was looking at him with genuine concern. But then neither did it seem likely that Olga Fiodorovna, with her love of beauty, would roll about on the dusty floor of an express train. Was it possible that he had been ravished by a random traveller? He wondered if he should confide in Bernard. Bernard would obviously have more experience of this sort of thing. If in fact he had been pestered by a complete stranger, oughtn't he perhaps to wash himself in disinfectant?

Olga Fiodorovna went upstairs to inspect her new accommodation and returned smiling. She had managed to procure a suite overlooking the Summer Gardens. It would of course cost a great many extra roubles, but that was unimportant. She led them through the hotel to the tradesmen's entrance at the rear where the car was waiting. Directing Bernard to sit in the back with Ashburner and Enid, she sat beside the driver. She was now wearing a long sable coat which she spread out on either side of her and stroked continually. Everyone assumed that Mr Karlovitch was either asleep or attending to his paperwork.

Before going to the Hermitage Museum they were driven to a cobbled street beside a canal to gaze at the house in which Pushkin had died. Olga Fiodorovna made them all get out, though she herself remained in the car. She wound down the window and shouted instructions at them. They must walk on to the middle of the bridge to feel the atmosphere of the place. The street was deserted and the canal frozen over. A black barge was caught in the ice.

'The duel was enacted over there,' she called, pointing into the distance. 'He was carried over the bridge and expired in the house.'

'Bugger Pushkin,' said Bernard.

'She must be awfully well off,' murmured Enid, looking enviously at Olga Fiodorovna's hand stabbing the air in its black leather glove. Enid was wearing woollen mittens. After only a few seconds she and Bernard hurried back to the car.

Ashburner lingered on the bridge. No longer conscious of the cold, he had the oddest feeling that he was all head, that his body had floated somewhere further off. Chin held at a curious angle, eyes shut, he stood in the attitude of a man straining to detect the enemy that stalked him. Snow collected on the shoulders of his overcoat. Then out of the silence in which he was so peculiarly suspended he heard the faint, high ring of steel on steel and louder, closer, the half-choked cry of a man run through.

Coming to himself, he fully understood that he had conjured up these sounds out of his mind. Nothing like it had ever happened to him before. In his case, he thought, lack of sleep was having a reverse effect. He had never felt so wide awake. Shaking the snow from his collar, he leant against the parapet and looked down at an old newspaper flapping on the surface of the canal. In that instant, caught in a gust of wind, the paper shifted, exposing the blackened leaves of a rotting cabbage. For some reason he was reminded of the white rug on the floor of the illustrator's studio, placed neither in front of the fireplace nor in the centre of the room.

'Mr Douglas,' called Olga Fiodorovna, 'we are waiting.'

The rug was necessary, thought Ashburner, retracing his steps. It was to cover some mark, some stain not yet removed.

He was silent in the car. They talked about him as if he wasn't there.

'I have a surprise for him in a little while,' said Olga Fiodorovna. 'Something of great importance. I feel he is not interested in paintings.'

'As long as it's not another visit to a metal worker,' Bernard said. 'He's up to here with metal workers.'

'He'll go down with pneumonia,' said Enid. 'He needs something for his head.'

The car stopped outside a palace. A soldier with a gun on his back walked up and down in front of a flight of monumental steps.

About to leave the car, Ashburner was told by Olga Fiodorovna to stay where he was. 'You are going somewhere else,' she said. She spoke to the driver who grunted and nodded his head. 'You are expected, Mr Douglas,' said Olga Fiodorovna. 'Professor Valentina Sochnikova will meet you at the door. There will be no need of an interpreter.'

'But where am I going?' asked Ashburner. He looked helplessly at the others and kept his hand on the door as if he might yet make a break for it.

'Search me,' said Bernard. 'It's supposed to be a surprise.'

Ashburner, whose whole existence since arriving on foreign soil had been a series of surprises, was dismayed at the news.

102

He couldn't bring himself to wave as he was driven away down the street.

The journey was short and ended outside a multi-storeyed building within an enclosed wall. The driver stayed at the wheel and indicated that Ashburner should get out. There were several cars and a white van parked in front of the entrance. Some slogan on the roof, insecurely battened, swung to and fro in the wind.

As soon as he set foot in the building, Ashburner knew he was in a hospital. There was no mistaking the tick from the clock on the gleaming wall, and the smells of ether and fear, surgical spirit and beeswax that filled the air he breathed. He was convinced he was going to see Nina. A small woman in white tennis shoes and a young man with a stethoscope dangling about his neck greeted him with affection; he was embraced by each in turn and kissed on both cheeks. Reluctantly removing his overcoat – the cleanliness of his surroundings made him conscious of his crumpled suit and his torn sleeve – he was led along a succession of tiled passages. It was only when he was ascending in the lift that it occurred to him that Nina couldn't possibly be here. They were four hundred miles from Moscow. He was still trying to work out what day it was and how many nights ago Nina had been spirited away when he found himself in a small ante-room, where he was handed a white coat and a cotton skull cap. Startled, he put them on and feeling like a pastry chef in a restaurant was directed through a green door with a red bulb burning above it.

He was in a dimly lit cubicle, alone, with a glass panel let into one wall. There were two television monitors in a corner, both screens blank, and in front of them an upright chair and a low tubular table on which was set an enamel basin and a paper towel. When he approached the glass panel and stared down, he saw that he was overlooking an operating theatre. A group of people, masked like terrorists, were hovering above a

103

naked figure spreadeagled on a raised black couch. Even as he watched, the angle of the couch altered and an attendant, steadying himself by placing his finger on the figure's cheekbone and his thumb on the peak of its shaved head, drew with a marking pen a freehand line in purple ink, bisecting the skull from ear to ear. The figure was so tormented with tubes and catheters, limbs so mangled with surgical apparatus, buttocks supported on a copper plate, flesh daubed with chemical dyes of livid green and yellow, that it was impossible to tell whether it was a man or a woman. Trembling with disgust and excitement, Ashburner retreated into a corner. Plainly he had been mistaken for Nina's husband, the brain specialist. The appalling prospect of being asked for his opinion, or worse, his assistance in the abattoir below, unmanned him.

He had no idea how long he stood there, cowering against the wall. The extreme silence in the sound-proofed room was in some way interfering with his breathing. He was just gathering his strength to wipe away the sweat that trickled into his eyes when the twin monitors flashed into colour and with the images on the screens came the frightful noise of a high-speed drill.

After a while, considerably calmer, for the piglet whine of the drill had shocked him into filling his lungs with air, Ashburner sat down and wiped his face with the paper towel. In close-up he viewed a hand in a glistening plastic glove wielding a scalpel. He couldn't see any gory fragments, or blood in tones of technicolor red, merely a pinkish pulp like the inside of a peach, palpitating beneath a strip of transparent gauze. Now that the barbarous reality beyond the glass panel had been transferred to that familiar, reassuring box, he watched the proceedings with interest.

In time, the gauze was removed and numerous pairs of slender silver scissors were inserted into the tissues and lifted and replaced with such rapidity that Ashburner was reminded

104

of a display of lace-making he had witnessed in Venice, given by an old woman in a doorway, the bobbins leaping like fish between her fingers. He could hear the magnified beat of a pulse and voices speaking in Russian and an unidentifiable crackling and rustling. Once he was shown, suspended from a steel armature, a pleated bladder sagging in and out like an accordion. The images on both screens were identical. He was in the middle of studying the probing of some tropical fruit, oyster grey and pink at the core, when quite suddenly the picture on the left-hand monitor wavered and slipped, to be replaced by a recognisably human chin and a mouth pegged cruelly open. Zooming in from above, the camera recorded a nose from whose nostril dangled a thin tube resembling a string of snot, and above it two eyes mercifully shut with white tape, and above the eyes a swollen band of forehead stained apricot yellow, in the centre of which and close to the hair-line, if the head had not been shaved, was the distinct impression of a star-shaped scar.

14

Following his collapse at the hospital – he was found lying in the passage outside the viewing cubicle – Ashburner was transported, wrapped in a cosy blanket, to his hotel. There he was helped to bed and slept for almost eighteen hours. Once or twice he imagined that he was visited by his wife and her Uncle Robert. Both of them reeked of chloroform.

When he finally awoke he saw Enid tiptoeing about the room. She told him everyone had been most concerned at his fainting like that. Mr Karlovitch had sent up a lavish bunch of tulips, but Olga Fiodorovna had given them to the chambermaid because she said they'd use up the oxygen. Bernard had popped in several times. Last night they had gone to a dinner given by the Artist's Union of Leningrad. They had come home early in order to keep an eye on him.

'I was just exhausted,' said Ashburner. 'All I needed was to get my head down.'

'Nina telephoned last night,' Enid said.

'You spoke to her, did you?' asked Ashburner.

'Olga did,' said Enid. 'Nina sent you her love.'

'How kind,' said Ashburner, and he lay back on the pillows.

At midday he dressed and was fetched downstairs by Bernard and taken to the restaurant. He drank a bowl of soup and ordered a large steak. 'Did you enjoy the Hermitage?' he asked politely.

'It was a bloody knockout,' said Bernard. 'I'm going back

106

there this afternoon. We were just hanging around to see how you were.'

'There was no need,' Ashburner said, but he was touched.

'Olga took me to the Botanical Gardens,' said Bernard. 'She insisted on showing me some plant with bloody big thorns all over it. She slipped up on her English, though – she said she wanted to show me the biggest prick in the Soviet Union. And you missed a good do last night. It was well up to standard. Karlovitch fell over. I even did some work this morning. I gave the guards the slip and nipped out for an hour before breakfast. I did a drawing of the Peter-Paul Fortress.'

'Jolly good,' said Ashburner. He couldn't think why Bernard was so keen on fortresses, particularly after his experience in Red Square.

'It's on the Neva,' explained Bernard. 'It was built to guard Russia's access to the Baltic.'

'I should have come with you,' said Ashburner. He thought his voice sounded uninterested. He tried to smile.

'You're sure you're all right now?' asked Bernard.

'Perfectly all right,' said Ashburner.

'You haven't got a dicky heart or anything, have you?' persisted Bernard.

'There's nothing wrong with my heart,' Ashburner said. He shifted uncomfortably on his chair. There was something else bothering him but he kept it to himself.

Olga Fiodorovna came into the restaurant and told Bernard she wanted a quiet word with Mr Douglas. 'Fire away,' said Bernard. 'I'll pretend I'm not here.'

She reminded him that they were going out in one hour. Perhaps he would be so good as to run along and see if Miss Dwyer was preparing himself. 'She is without means of telling the time,' she said.

Muttering, Bernard took his cup of coffee to another table and sat with his back to them.

'You will understand,' began Olga Fiodorovna, 'that I am

107

responsible for your welfare. I do not wish to sound like a schoolmistress with a recalcitrant pupil. I speak from the heart and not from malice. I think you understand what I mean.'

'Quite,' said Ashburner, though he was totally foxed.

'I will tell you a little parable, Mr Douglas. You may have noticed that I am not myself. I have had problems, domestic matters that have affected me.' She moved a plate irritatingly around the tablecoth. 'I am very sensitive, too sensitive perhaps. You had a mother?'

'Yes, of course,' said Ashburner.

'Then you will understand. My mother is very Russian, very beautiful, very impulsive. When I was a small girl she would hug me so passionately that I would cry out. If I did not eat up my food she would shake me. It was for my own good, you understand. She wanted me to have my vitamins.'

Ashburner was a little out of his depth. He had been sent away to school when he was seven and his own mother was something of a stranger. Her hugs, such as they were, could be described as lukewarm.

Suddenly Olga Fiodorovna leaned across the table and seizing hold of his upper jaw between thumb and forefinger, painfully squeezed it. 'Eat, eat, eat,' she cried, increasing the pressure cruelly. Abruptly she released him. 'But now,' she continued, 'it is I who am in charge of my little Mamotchka. She is very old and refuses to swallow her food. Things have swung full circle.' Holding an imaginary fork, she stabbed it in the direction of Ashburner's mouth.

Alarmed, he pushed his chair further back from the table. She was certainly very like her mother, he thought.

'We are all responsible for one another,' said Olga Fiodorovna. 'I think you have a strongly developed sense of duty. Am I right?'

'Absolutely,' he agreed. He knew she was humouring him.

'I think you are sensitive like me, Mr Douglas. For people

108

with an artistic temperament, life is not easy. You recognise more than most your duty to yourself, your dependents, your country.'

'You may be right,' he said. He thought she was overdoing the patriotic bit. He wondered whether, in slyly mentioning his dependents, she was alluding to his wife. He felt ashamed, and then he remembered that she was always mistaking him for someone else.

'Though of course,' said Olga Fiodorovna, 'duty shouldn't preclude a sense of fun.'

'Fun!' he said.

'It is advisable, however, to keep one's high spirits within bounds, particularly in a country other than one's own.'

'I don't quite follow you,' said Ashburner stiffly. 'In what way have I been high-spirited?'

The interpreter looked him firmly in the eye. 'There have been reports,' she said, 'of pranks at the home of Mr Shabelsky's friends.'

'I was savaged by a dog,' he contested. 'It was hardly an occasion for high spirits.'

'The manager of the Peking hotel,' Olga Fiodorovna told him, 'received a complaint from a woman guest on the same floor as yourself.'

'I admit it,' Ashburner cried triumphantly. 'But the reasons for such a step were beyond reproach.'

He thought she was being very unreasonable. Though pale, he no longer looked like a man on the run. The plaster had gone from the bridge of his nose and the scratch had almost healed. He had at last changed his clothes and was now wearing a tweed jacket and a pair of crumpled flannel trousers. About to argue with her, pull her down a peg or two, he recollected that he was obligated both to the interpreter and to her employers and it would be a breach of good manners to justify himself. If nothing else, he thought, he still had a fair idea of what's what.

109

It was only when Enid came downstairs that Olga Fiodorovna sprang it on them that they were scheduled to visit the Piskarevsky cemetery, built to commemorate the six hundred thousand Russians who had perished in the Siege of Leningrad.

'That's all very well,' protested Bernard, 'but I'm supposed to be an artist, not a bloody vicar. I don't want to see any graves.' He was disgusted and flatly refused to go. He had, he said, every intention of returning to the Hermitage Museum. 'I've only looked at one tenth of the paintings,' he complained. 'It's potty to come all this way and not spend more time there.'

'Who worked out where we should go?' asked Enid. 'Does everyone visit the cemetery?'

'Not everybody,' admitted Olga Fiodorovna. 'Dignitaries from the armed forces, statesmen.' She was on the point of adding that in this particular instance it had been Mrs St Clair who had expressed a wish to go there, when she remembered how the mention of her name seemed peculiarly to distress Mr Douglas. He was badly affected by his separation from her.

'I'd love to go to the cemetery,' said Ashburner. He didn't want to crawl, but he thought Bernard had gone a little too far. It was like somebody speaking scathingly of the cenotaph in Whitehall.

Olga Fiodorovna was in a dilemma. It wasn't possible that Mr Douglas should wander about on his own, but then neither could she allow Mr Burns out of her sight. The fact that Mr Douglas was apparently the more extrovert of the two didn't prove anything. It was early days.

'I think I'd like to go to the cemetery,' said Enid. 'I often go to the one at Highgate.' She had once wandered into a churchyard, by mistake, on the island of Crete, in which the bodies had been left lying in open pits, under sacking. Tacked to pieces of driftwood were passport photographs of the deceased in life, all of them staring as though surprised by ghosts. She hadn't seen much, just the odd boot sticking out, but the sea was quite near and it was very hot and she was wearing shorts, and it was a disturbing thing to stumble upon under a blazing sky.

'I will ask for another interpreter,' said Olga Fiodorovna, making a decision. 'She is quite a nice lady, called Valentina, who will explain to you the facts of the cemetery. I will accompany Mr Burns to the Hermitage.' She went away to make her arrangements.

Ashburner apologised to Bernard for landing him with Olga. 'But as you may have guessed,' he said, 'I'm not terribly keen on Art. And it would be better for me if I was in the open air.'

He longed to have a man's talk with Bernard, but it wasn't the right moment. In the circumstances it would be easier if they were alone.

Bernard told him not to worry, he could handle Olga. She wasn't only stunning to look at but bright into the bargain. 'You just have to keep her off the subject of her Mum,' he said. He didn't know if it was all that wise, Ashburner being taken off to gaze at a load of tombstones. It was pretty morbid, carting him from hospital to grave.

Valentina, the hired help, wasn't as good at her job as Olga Fiodorovna. Twice Enid pointed at buildings and enquired what they were and both times Valentina said she didn't know. She seemed nervous and she wasn't suitably dressed for the weather. Her coat was thin and she wore high-heeled court shoes over woollen ankle socks. She kept repeating that they mustn't stay long at the cemetery. Miss Fiodorovna had ordered her to be brisk; in the evening the English visitors were going to the Opera.

After half an hour's driving the car stopped. Ashburner had expected a church, but all he saw was a concrete blockhouse and a turnstile and, beyond, a flat white landscape cut with

111

symmetrical paths swept clear of snow and edged with withered shrubs encased in envelopes of polythene to protect them from the frost. Between the paths jutted squares of polished granite, identical in size and each one no larger than a box of chocolates, planted row upon row, stretching endlessly to the horizon. Under glass cloches lay cardboard scrolls, printed with names and numbers, tilted to the sky. The place had the appearance of a garden centre closed for the winter. It was bitterly cold.

Enid told Ashburner he should tie Nina's pink scarf round his head, turban fashion, to cover his ears.

He said it wasn't necessary, but then almost immediately he took it from his pocket and did as she suggested.

'It makes you rather Indian,' said Enid, but she was being kind; she thought he looked like a brutal housewife.

Valentina, shuddering in the icy wind, garbled a melancholy account of death by torture, bombardment, hypothermia and starvation. Orchestral music, relayed from loudspeakers, regulated their steps to a funeral pace as they marched along the path.

'The music helps,' said Enid. 'It makes it sadder.'

'They've got piped music in my local supermarket now,' Ashburner told her. 'I don't find it altogether helpful.'

There was nothing really to see, nothing dramatic to catch the eye.

'They should have marble angels,' said Enid, close to tears. 'And crosses and ornamental urns.' She would have liked to have taken her time, wept, let her mind form pictures of the dead and the manner of their dying, but Valentina was racing ahead, her stout legs whipped purple, desperate to get it over with.

'Nina would have wanted to come here,' said Ashburner. 'I suppose being an artist she's more capable of appreciating this sort of thing.'

'I'm not being bitchy,' said Enid, 'but Nina's not all that

good, you know. I mean, she hasn't progressed. Not since she started fiddling about with metal.'

'I'm not much of a judge,' Ashburner said. 'But I saw one or two still-lifes in her drawing room. I thought they were charming.'

'She did those when she was a student,' said Enid.

'Still,' persisted Ashburner, 'it proves it's in her. And she's remarkably astute about people, about situations.'

'I don't see her like you do,' said Enid. 'But then I'm a woman.'

They had reached the end of the path and were ready to turn right to approach the second avenue when they realised that Valentina was already hurrying back along the way they had come.

'I don't want to go yet,' said Enid mutinously. 'We haven't seen anything.'

Ashburner said the poor girl was obviously freezing to death – and besides, one path was very like another. He took hold of Enid's arm and trotted her unwillingly in pursuit. He wondered if all artistic women were strong-minded.

They found Valentina cowering in the doorway of the blockhouse. Enid asked her whether there was a plaque anywhere that stated who had killed all these people. Valentina told her that there was a stone obelisk at the far end of the cemetery which gave the dates and details of the Siege.

'Yes, but does it mention the Germans?' said Enid.

'We Russians,' Valentina asserted, 'do not like to keep old wounds alive.'

'My God,' cried Enid, 'you should do. You can't keep all this going and then pretend you don't remember who caused it.'

Valentina looked uncomfortable. Ashburner was about to whisper tactfully the words 'East Germany' into Enid's ear when he saw a woman in a fur coat, who until that moment had been walking in the company of an old man and a child, leave the central cinder path and begin to pick her way between the memorial tables in the snow. She wore a small pill-box hat perched on the top of her head from which escaped a quantity of thick black hair. The child set up a loud wailing.

Ashburner ran down the path, waving his arms and shouting. The woman didn't turn round but she too began to run, leaping over the stones and holding on to her hat. The pink scarf blew from Ashburner's head and rolled across the snow. Retrieving it, he looked up and found that the woman had disappeared. The old man and the child were walking hand in hand into the distance.

'What was all that about?' said Enid, when Ashburner returned.

'I thought I saw someone I knew,' he said.

'Who?' she asked.

'A woman colleague of mine from the office,' he lied.

'Funny,' she said. 'I would have thought you'd have run in the opposite direction.'

15

They arrived late at the Kirov Theatre. It was Mr Karlovitch's fault; he'd been unavoidably delayed at an important function. The metal workers of Leningrad, he said, had given a luncheon in memory of a colleague volted into the grave by an incorrectly wired buffing machine.

In the car, Olga Fiodorovna had a word with him. She spoke in Russian, but it was obvious she was ticking him off. By the time they had deposited their coats in the cloakroom the curtain had already risen.

'Let us be as inconspicuous as possible,' suggested Olga Fiodorovna, hastening them along a corridor.

Ashburner wasn't expecting to enjoy himself. He considered theatre-going an overrated pastime and dreadfully expensive. If there was anything on worth seeing, his wife usually left him at home and took her friend Caroline. He was acquainted with the story of Faust, having as a sixth-former marginally preferred Marlowe to Goethe, and it wasn't his idea of a good night out, particularly if it was going to be sung aloud. But within moments of entering the opulent auditorium and hearing the thunderous accompaniment of the orchestra and the melancholy voices of the scholars soaring to the painted ceiling of the theatre, he was transported backwards in time to an occasion, until now totally forgotten, when as a child of six or seven he had been taken on a trolley bus by his grandmother to a pantomime at the Angel, Islington. Then, as now, the audience had overflowed into the aisles and even crouched on the steps on either side of the proscenium arch. How many other things had he forgotten, he thought worriedly, but then in spite of himself the recollection of that long ago outing was so pleasurable that he began to smile broadly.

Elbowing and shoving, exchanging angry repartee every step of the way, Olga Fiodorovna herded her charges down the centre aisle and along the edge of the orchestra pit, draped in scarlet plush and looped with golden ropes, and up the second gangway under the overhang of the rococo balconies, until, leaving a trail of disturbed patrons in their wake, she brought them to a large box overlooking the stage. Inside sat a party of young people, some studying the score, some peacefully waving opera glasses in time to the music. Olga Fiodorovna fetched an attendant and produced her documents. She whispered at the top of her voice. The rows of upturned faces watching the spectacle on the stage swivelled to watch the spectacle in the box. The original occupants, outmaneuvered by superior permits, stumbled away into the darkness.

'It had to be done,' hissed Olga Fiodorovna. 'We were within our rights.'

Ashburner, jostling unsuccessfully with Mr Karlovitch for possession of a seat next to Enid and as far away from the interpreter as possible, sank into a velvet-covered chair and leaned against the edge of the rail.

On stage a Good Angel, large and motherly-looking, was trying to persuade Faustus to think things over. Faustus, bent over his books, was listening half-heartedly. His mind was altogether made up. He was wearing high-heeled boots, the necessity for which became apparent when Mephistopheles materialised in a belch of sulphuric smoke and Faustus leapt to his feet; he was smaller than Enid and spherical in shape. The voice of Mephistopheles was deep and powerful, and he seemed to have the better tunes. Faustus' voice was high and complaining, and he never got going long enough to break into

116

a cadenza. At the end of every intonation he walked a few paces or swept round in a tottering circle, dragging his cloak behind him and staring haughtily at the audience through a haze of spiralling dust which, caught in the dazzle of the footlights, sparkled like fireflies. In spite of the absurd convention of setting words to music and the comical appearance of Faustus, Ashburner was chilled by the scene. Though the libretto was in Russian, he knew that Mephistopheles, in answer to Faustus' question as to the location of hell, was bound to reply: *Hell hath no limits. But where we are is Hell, and where Hell is there must we be. And to be short, when all the world dissolves, all places shall be Hell that is not Heaven.* Ashburner hadn't been a religious schoolboy, any more than he was a religious man, but he had found it easy to memorise and retain that particular portion of the text. Perhaps, he thought, it had something to do with the repetitive use of the swear-word. His wife's idea of hell was a wet day on the beach at Nevin. His concentration, already waning, entirely left him when Faustus, having completed his pact with Lucifer and now in a position to obtain anything in the universe, demanded a wife. It would have been more in the order of priorities, Ashburner thought, to have asked for an extra three inches in height. Glancing away from the stage and puzzling in his mind as to what for him constituted a hellish place, his gaze fell on a plaster cherub on the far side of the auditorium, holding aloft a torch. Directly beneath the cherub sat Nina.

He was so certain that it was she that he seized hold of Olga Fiodorovna's arm and cried out 'Quick'. He took his eyes off Nina for perhaps a fraction of a second and yet, when he looked again she had gone and in her place sat a man wearing horn-rimmed spectacles.

'Are you unwell?' asked Olga Fiodorovna. She peered into his face and, fearing he might faint, fanned him with her documents.

'What's wrong?' whispered Enid, bending forward intimately across the lap of Mr Karlovitch.

'A slight touch of cramp,' said Ashburner, and after massaging his calf in a realistic manner he pretended to be engrossed in the singing.

He daren't look into the body of the auditorium. She was there somewhere, of that he was sure, but he would lose her if he turned round. Like Lot's wife she would be transformed into a pillar of salt. Cunning was essential. He couldn't attempt to understand why she was carrying on in this mysterious fashion, but he was certain that she wasn't hiding from him of her own volition. Had this been England he might have dismissed her behaviour as nothing out of the ordinary – and anyway he'd have been far too busy rushing home to feed the dog to dwell on it, beyond feeling irritated. He had once telephoned her at her studio and she'd impersonated a Japanese. He'd known it was she but Nina wouldn't give in; she'd kept saying she was velly solly but Mrs St Clair was away. But it was quite another thing to act the fool abroad. In many ways they were alike – that was why he'd been drawn to her in the first place. Except when dealing with him she had very good manners and was something of a coward. He feared she was being manipulated by others and was in serious danger. He had learnt in the last three days that death itself wasn't a problem. He would never again torture himself with images of his wife's funeral. It was waiting for death that was unbearable. He was so agitated that he trembled all over and had to bite his lip to stop his teeth from chattering.

During the interval they went down into the foyer.

Olga Fiodorovna insisted on fetching him a cup of water. She was gone for ten minutes and when she returned and handed him the cup her gesture was so reminiscent of his own at the airport, when Nina had complained of feeling rotten, that he spilled most of the water down the front of his suit. Mr Karlovitch asked them to excuse him; he was leaving early to

118

accept an important telephone call from Georgia. He took the cloakroom tickets from his pocket and gave them to the interpreter. They began to discuss something in Russian.

'You don't look well, Douglas,' said Enid. 'Why don't you go home in the cab with Vladimir?'

'I'm enjoying myself enormously,' Ashburner said. He couldn't think who Vladimir was. He told Enid that he had come here once with his grandmother. He realised he was talking nonsense, but there was so much noise all around them that he didn't think she had heard. He was saying anything that came into his head because he was actually concentrating on a man and a woman who were standing behind Bernard. They kept glancing in his direction, though perhaps they were only interested in his clothes.

'Why don't *you* go home with Vladimir,' said Bernard, nudging Enid. 'From where I was sitting you were watching damn all on stage.' He was so hemmed in by the crowd that he was forced, between puffs, to hold his cigarette straight up in the air like an umbrella.

Ashburner was waiting for Nina to approach him, either directly or through an emissary. Several people pressed against him, men and women, but it was accidental and on account of the crush. Nobody slipped anything into his palm. 'They know we're foreigners,' he said. 'How d'you suppose they call tell?'

'It could have something to do with us speaking a foreign language,' said Bernard. He agreed with Enid. Ashburner's behaviour was a bit rum, rambling on about his grandma, scrutinising faces, rubbing up against women. If he wasn't careful someone would come over and thump him. Perhaps he was running a fever.

Returning to the auditorium, Ashburner followed Enid down the centre aisle. He gazed upwards at the balconies curving in a semi-circle to meet the ornate boxes that climbed in tiers to the painted ceiling, and feigned an interest in the

119

architecture. He hoped that by moving his head about he would be more visible to Nina if she were watching him. He had reached the orchestra pit and was just about to turn away when out of the corner of his eye he saw her, seated in the circle box between two men. She was laughing and pushing the hair back from her forehead.

He continued to pursue Enid, neither faltering in his stride nor altering the expression on his face. Knowing that at any moment the second act would begin, he loitered in the aisle as if held back by the crowd until, the lights dimming and the orchestra striking up, he shouldered his way into the passage and sprinting like a madman round the back of the auditorium leapt up the stairs to the circle. All sense of caution had left him. Panting, he blundered through the velvet curtains. A blast of trumpets heralded the entrance of the Pope on stage, escorted by cardinals.

Bernard was thinking about Sickert – all those studies he'd done of the interiors of theatres. In the right hands, pastels were better than oils. He looked up, distracted by figures swaying in the box on the opposite side of the proscenium arch. He was amazed to see Ashburner, bald head catching the light, grappling with two men.

Olga Fiodorovna treated Ashburner sympathetically. In the car she patted his hand and refrained from uttering a word of reproach. Nor did she ask him for an explanation. At the hotel she suggested he go straight to bed; she would have a glass of hot milk sent up to him.

As soon as he reached his room, Ashburner telephoned Bernard. There was no reply. He waited for his milk, poured it down the lavatory and rang Bernard again. Thinking he might be in the bar, he went downstairs and was just in time to see him going out of the front door of the hotel. Collecting his coat from the cloakroom, he hurried in pursuit. The lamps had been torn out of the ground and but for a fitful moon he might have come to grief traversing the battlefield of the street.

From a distant thoroughfare he heard the occasional rumble of traffic. When he turned the corner Bernard was already crossing the deserted square, limping purposefully towards the ornamental gates of the Summer Gardens. Breaking into a run, Ashburner caught up with him.

'I do apologise,' he said, 'but I must talk to you.' But he couldn't, not immediately; he didn't know where to begin or how to express himself.

They entered the Gardens and strolled in silence along a moonlit avenue between linden trees.

'It's difficult to put into words,' said Ashburner at last. 'It's this worry about Nina, and there's something else –'

'What were you doing in that box with those men?' asked Bernard.

'I thought I saw Nina,' Ashburner said. 'I keep seeing her. She was in the cemetery this afternoon. I recognised her hair. I saw her at the hospital too. I imagined she was on the operating table. Her head was shaved.'

'She's got a remarkable rate of recovery then,' said Bernard. 'Not to mention hair growth.'

'I've become peculiarly sensitive,' Ashburner said. 'It's most unlike me. But you know on the bridge – when we went to look at the place where that fellow Pushkin died – I distinctly heard the sound of clashing swords. Isn't that ridiculous?'

'Yes,' said Bernard. 'Considering they fought with pistols.'

'I know it's absurd,' Ashburner said. 'I don't know what's come over me.' He was about to add that he wasn't much good at travelling alone – that his wife usually handled things, held their passports while he dealt with the luggage, spoke the odd word of French if called upon – when he thought better of it. Though it was true that if his wife had been travelling with him he wouldn't have landed in his present predicament, he sensed that Bernard would find such an excuse pathetic. He peered through the trees at something bulky on a pedestal,

121

encased in wood. 'Is that a gun installation?' he asked.

'It's a statue,' Bernard said. 'They board them up in winter so the cold doesn't crack them.'

'Don't you find it sinister?' blurted Ashburner. 'I mean, sending me off to watch that operation? They know perfectly well I'm not Nina's husband. They may have been confused at the beginning, but they must have worked it out by now.'

'You forget where you are,' Bernard said. 'This is the most bureaucracy-ridden country in the world. They issued a permit for a visiting Englishman to go to a hospital. It didn't matter if it was the wrong Englishman. They couldn't cancel the original bit of paper – it would have buggered up the computer.' He flung his cigarette into the darkness.

'There's more to it,' persisted Ashburner. 'I've been giving a lot of thought to it. It began that day we went to the illustrator's studio. Olga kept running off and leaving us stranded in the car. For no reason she disappeared into a block of flats. You weren't there. You'd been awkward, if you remember, about going shopping. Enid and I were chatting about mothers. Shortly afterwards a car drove up and some men got out and followed Olga into the same building. One of them was carrying a suitcase. My point is, it could have been Nina's.'

'Nina had two suitcases,' Bernard reminded him. 'She brought my coat in one of them.' He seemed to be listening for something. Coming to a wrought-iron bench at the side of the path, he sat down abruptly and glanced backwards into the darkness. 'If it was anybody's suitcase,' he said, 'it was probably yours.'

'That hadn't occurred to me,' admitted Ashburner. He felt stupidly crestfallen. A gust of wind blew through the trees, showering him with snow.

'Look, mate,' Bernard said. 'Take it from me, nothing funny's going on. Nina's fine. She's not been liquidated. She rang yesterday evening.' He held his arm up in the moonlight

122

and studied his wristwatch. 'At this moment she's on the midnight express from Moscow.'

'That's the other thing,' said Ashburner. Carefully, because he wanted Bernard to believe him and he knew he must be lucid, he told of his experience on the train. Once or twice he expressed himself crudely so that Bernard wouldn't lose interest. When he had finished he was mortified to find that Bernard was laughing, silently at first, doubled up over his knees on the bench as though in pain, and then out loud. The noise of his laughter rolled through the moonlit wastes of the glacial Summer Gardens.

'I'm afraid,' said Ashburner, 'that I don't take these things as lightly as you do. I didn't enjoy it. I don't want to preach, but personally speaking I have to feel some modicum of affection in order to gain any satisfaction.'

Bernard snorted uncontrollably.

'Satisfaction apart,' shouted Ashburner, 'I now feel rather uncomfortable. One or two things are not quite ship-shape.' Suddenly realising the absurdity of bellowing such intimate confidences in the middle of the night in a foreign land, he too began to snigger. Controlling himself, he lowered his voice and described the strange symptoms that had bothered him since the morning. 'I'm probably imagining it,' he said. 'But I thought that you, being a man of the world, might advise me.'

Bernard had never known anyone like Ashburner – not to spend time with. The man looked and spoke like a civil servant; yet he was obviously insanely romantic. It wasn't so extraordinary after all that Nina had taken up with him. She was basically a rather bossy girl who should have married somebody inadequate and produced a crop of children. Art didn't do anything for her. She only mucked about with it because the brain specialist was a total egotist and she was left too much on her own. Perhaps Ashburner was made for her. If so, beyond getting all worked up emotionally, he'd be able to take the truth.

123

Clinically he explained to Ashburner that his little bit of leg-over on the train couldn't be responsible for his present symptoms. He had probably become infected ten days ago. Drinking so heavily had probably aggravated the condition. He must take the pills Nina had put in his suitcase, one a day for five days. And he must cut out the drink. He patted Ashburner on the shoulder and told him not to worry. It wasn't anything to write home about. His private parts weren't about to drop off. Most of the people he knew either had it or were about to get it.

Ashburner said nothing for some time. He sat slumped on the bench, his chin sunk on his chest. He was both mystified and relieved by Bernard's medical lecture.

'Have I been infectious for ten days?' he asked at last.

'More or less,' said Bernard.

'How will I tell my wife?' said Ashburner. He didn't feel guilty or upset about her. She seemed to have receded into the past. He wondered how he would ever find his way back to her.

'You don't,' Bernard said. 'You nip round to your doctor when you go home, ask him for some more pills and pop them in her morning tea. And hide the booze from her.'

'She doesn't drink,' said Ashburner, and he stood up. They began to walk along the path towards the gates. Keeping pace with them and somewhere to their right, footsteps crunched the snow beneath the linden trees.

'It's old Karlovitch,' murmured Bernard. 'Keeping tabs on us.'

Ashburner didn't find it all that objectionable. Mother Russia sprawled eight million square miles across the surface of the earth, from the Baltic Sea to the Pacific Ocean, from the borders of tropical Persia to the ice-floes of the North Pole. A few yards' surveillance, he thought philosophically, was neither here nor there.

124

16

The aeroplane descended between mountain peaks into the valley of Tblisi. Mr Karlovitch pointed out an artificial sea to the north, but nobody looked. Flying to Georgia had proved a nightmare for Bernard; he hadn't been allowed to smoke.

They stepped down from the grey aircraft into blinding sunlight. The President of the Artists' Union of the Tblisi district, surrounded by a retinue of committee members, was there to greet them. Shimmering behind a heat haze, the welcoming delegation rippled across the tarmac, holding tulips and smoking little fat cigars. The President was tall and imposing with a Hapsburg chin; he resembled, or so Enid thought, a police inspector in a French film. He wore, slung casually round his shoulders, a white mackintosh with epaulets.

They drove in convoy through the old quarter of the town to a Hilton-style hotel built on a plateau landscaped with oleanders and magnolias and were immediately taken up to the fifteenth floor for luncheon, though it was four o'clock in the afternoon. There, plied with glasses of champagne and urged to eat pieces of charcoal-flavoured mutton and unleavened bread stuffed with goat's cheese, they listened to fulsome speeches, doggedly translated by a wilting Olga Fiodorovna. The sun beat against the picture window of the restaurant. Suffocating in their winter woollies, laps strewn with mutilated tulips, the fêted guests wiped the perspiration from their smiling faces and nibbled quantities of onion salad sprinkled with basil. Outside the window spread the roofs of ancient houses and the domes of Byzantine churches. In a small park lay a man and a dog, flopped out on the withered grass. High above the churches and houses and park dangled a cable car, its overhead wires catching the sunlight, strung in a glittering loop from the slopes of the town to the top of Mount Mtatsminda. Across the blue horizon, peaks buttered with snow, rolled the Caucasian Range.

The President wished his visitors to know that an exciting itinerary had been prepared. They would be anxious to see a collective farm and possibly a famous painter. In particular, Mrs St Clair had asked to meet the metal workers of Tblisi. At the mention of Nina's name, Ashburner started violently. The committee regretted that Mrs St Clair was still unwell and hoped that she would soon fly, restored to health, into the arms of Mother Georgia.

Taking everyone by surprise, Ashburner lurched to his feet. Aware that he cut a dishevelled figure – his old school tie undone and hanging like a dormant snake from his collar – he none the less felt compelled to reply. 'The warmth of our welcome,' he began, 'is typical of the Soviet Union. We are looking forward to seeing something of your beautiful countryside and your metal workers. Were my wife at my side, she too would assure you of our friendship and our gratitude.' He had thought to say more. It had been in his mind, before he mentioned his wife, to liken the landscape to certain regions of Spain, though his visit to Santander had been brief and he wasn't sure if the comparison was diplomatic, politically speaking. Confused, he sat down; he hadn't been thinking of his wife at all, but of Nina.

Across the table, the President rested his elbow on Bernard's shoulder. Already sinking under the heat, Bernard wagged a belligerent finger at Olga Fiodorovna, who was

126

fanning herself with the hotel reservations. 'No offence meant,' he cried, 'but I'm not going near a collective farm. I don't care how you put it, but make that clear to them.'

'You will not be forced to visit a collective farm, Mr Burns. I do not have to make it clear.'

'Same goes for metal workers,' Bernard warned her. 'If I set eyes on one I'll go for him with a blow torch.'

'There are some interesting churches in Tblisi,' Olga told him soothingly. 'They are very old, very historical.'

'No churches,' snapped Bernard. 'I want to see where Stalin was born, and I want to go to the pictures.'

The President looked enquiringly at Olga Fiodorovna but she pretended not to notice. 'We are going perhaps tomorrow,' she said. 'There is a very famous painter living nearby in a very –'

'Moving pictures,' said Bernard. 'The flicks, the movies, the cinema. Get it?'

Enid had overheard Bernard shouting out the word 'Stalin' and was alarmed at his outspokenness. None of them, until now, had brought up names. They hadn't mentioned Solzhenitsyn or Nabokov or Trotsky, or even that ballet dancer. She herself, in a suitably concerned tone of voice – she hadn't been giggling or anything like that – had asked Olga Fiodorovna how Mr Brezhnev was. She had thought it only polite. When they had left England the newspapers were reporting him as practically dead. Olga's reply had made her feel like a scandal-monger and a liar; she'd said brusquely that Mr Brezhnev was as fit as a fiddle, or words to that effect. Altogether she gave the impression that it wasn't done to talk about Mr Brezhnev, alive or dead. Nobody had told them it wouldn't be tactful to bring up names. There really hadn't been the opportunity; they'd been far too busy discussing Ashburner's suitcase or his tangle with that dog in the bathroom, or his fainting fit at the hospital or his night at the opera. For someone so ordinary and boring, it was astonishing how much time they spent talking about Ashburner.

'The others can do as they damn well please,' said Bernard, lopsided under the weight of the President's mighty arm. Both men were puffing on cigarettes, blowing clouds of smoke up to the ceiling and coughing.

'He ought to lie down,' Enid said. 'We all need to lie down.'

But already Olga Fiodorovna was gathering her papers together and explaining to the Committee that her charges must rest.

They retired to their rooms on the nineteenth floor. Enid and Bernard lay on pillows on their balconies and soaked up the sun. Ashburner dozed on his divan bed. Though he was frightfully tired he found it difficult to sleep. He now had a sore throat, and he imagined he had a slight pain in his chest. He would have liked to telephone Bernard, but he didn't know what room to call. Lying there, listening to the faint din of crockery and cutlery below, he suddenly heard Enid's voice. 'I haven't sent any post cards,' she said.

Startled, he got up and went out on to the balcony. Leaning over the rail and peering sideways, he saw a white brassière draped upon the adjacent balustrade.

'Oh, you're there,' he cried heartily. He didn't want her to suppose he'd been playing Peeping Tom.

'Isn't it glorious?' called Enid. 'Isn't this the life?'

'Rather,' he said, staring out over the town; the sun had certainly put his hat on. He had always been known as a man who appreciated a beautiful view. Indeed on more than one occasion his wife had threatened to scream if he went on once more about this line of hillside or that stretch of coast. He had sat for hours in his sou'wester on the beach at Nevin, watching the sun sink into the sea and the moon float up over the headland, knowing that soon he would go indoors and light the fire and tell his wife of the beauties of that self-same sunset and moonrise. He realised it wasn't just a question of his physical indisposition, this despondency of mood. It simply

128

wasn't the same, being on one's own with no one to go home to. It was true that it all looked splendid out there; it was almost sublime, all those little crooked streets and that big mountain and the scent of magnolias drifting up from the plateau below. If this building collapses from shoddy workmanship, he thought, I won't stand a chance. Somewhere to his left he heard Bernard's voice, complaining that he had run out of matches.

'Heavens,' said Ashburner. 'We're like a tin of sardines.' Fetching a chair from his room he clambered on to it and looked over the top of the concrete partition.

'For Christ's sake,' snarled Bernard. 'Go away and lie down.' He was spread naked on the mosaic floor.

'I'm so sorry,' Ashburner said. 'I just wanted a word.' He stepped back off the chair and prowled about his room, sneaking glances at himself in the dressing-table mirror. He was sure he had put on weight. He pulled his stomach in as far as he could; the bulge shifted to his diaphragm. At this rate he wouldn't be able to take his jacket off, let alone his shirt. Bernard didn't appear to have an ounce of fat on him, though that was hardly an excuse for taking all his clothes off. He tried and failed to remember the last time he had lain naked anywhere, not to mention in broad daylight. The very last time had probably been forty-five years ago on the bathroom floor, and even then he'd most likely had his bottom slapped for it. Some men made awful fools of themselves. The sights he'd seen on the Lido last summer in Venice!

'What sort of a word?' called Bernard, but Ashburner refused to answer.

Enid was the first to go downstairs. She saw some postcards under a glass tray and would have bought them if anyone had been behind the counter. Disappointed, she sauntered through the cool reception hall in her pink summer dress with the sweetheart neck and emerged into the evening sunshine. She stood at the kerb looking down at the flight of steps banked by flowering shrubs and the road that wound beneath. On the far side of the street she could see a row of shops and people walking up and down carrying string bags and pushing prams. There didn't appear to be any zebra crossings or belisha beacons, or any way of getting from one side of the road to the other without running the risk of being knocked down by the cars and lorries that rumbled in either direction. Even as she watched, a man stepped off the opposite pavement and ran zigzagging through the traffic. A dog followed him. Reaching the kerb the man sprinted up the slope towards the back of the hotel. At that moment a fleet of cars roared up the ramp, narrowly missing the dog who, streaking under the front fender of the leading vehicle, sprang up the bank to safety and bounded away through the oleander bushes. With a tremendous slamming of doors a dozen members of the Committee of the Artists' Union left their cars and marshalled themselves behind the President. Athletically, white mackintosh swinging from his shoulders, he began to leap two at a time up the steps. Enid ran back inside the hotel.

Ashburner stuck by Mr Karlovitch. They sat in easy chairs beside a rubber plant in a shadowy corner of the reception hall. Unlike Bernard, who could have been mistaken for a member of the committee, strutting up and down in plimsols and ridiculously narrow white trousers, Mr Karlovitch still wore his sombre city suit, though he had removed his knitted scarf.

'Any idea what's on the agenda?' Ashburner called to Enid, but she was vivaciously communicating, by means of sign language and exaggerated facial expressions, with a young man in a panama hat and she didn't hear him. Nobody appeared in a hurry to go anywhere. But for the absence of drinks it might have seemed that a cocktail party was in progress.

'Who are all these people?' demanded Ashburner. He couldn't remember seeing any of them before, except possibly

130

the tall fellow with the weak chin. Most of them were dressed up as gangsters in black cotton shirts and floppy white ties.

'Artists,' Mr Karlovitch told him. 'Sculptors, poets, friends.' He pointed along the hall. 'You are wanted,' he said.

'Mr Douglas,' shouted Olga Fiodorovna. 'You are requested on the telephone.'

Ashburner ran in a dreadful state of agitation towards her; he thought it was a phone call from England. 'Hurry,' urged the interpreter. 'It is Mrs St Clair for you. The connection is not good.'

'Hallo, hallo,' he said breathlessly. 'Can you hear me?'

A voice, distorted by static interference, spoke in a foreign tongue.

'Are you there?' he cried.

Olga Fiodorovna was walking away. Everyone was flowing out of the hall to the front entrance.

'Hallo, hallo,' he shouted desperately. 'Douglas Ashburner here.' He felt in his bones the appalling distances that separated him from Nina. He was the telegraph wire itself, strung out across the steppes of Mother Russia, buried under rivers, affected by tropical rains and arctic storms. 'Hallo, hallo,' he repeated hopelessly, knowing she would never hear him. The line went dead.

In the car, wedged between total strangers, it seemed to him that his life had been sabotaged by unknown persons. He had no idea with whom he was travelling; cigarette smoke swirled about him like a fog.

They arrived at a newly built cinema erected in the middle of an industrial site.

'This is something different, isn't it?' cried Bernard, delighted that he had got his own way, though in fact the place bore a resemblance to the no man's land outside the hotel in Leningrad. Picking their way between slabs of concrete and abandoned machinery and kicking up clouds of white dust, they approached the entrance. Two ladies had mysteriously joined them. Both were extremely tall and well built, with broad foreheads decorated with kiss-curls. Clad in identical leather mini skirts they sashayed over the rubble, escorted by the President.

The cinema was empty and smelt of damp concrete. The walls hadn't yet been painted. A number of cables dangled from the ceiling. Olga Fiodorovna sat next to Ashburner. The moment he had settled she seized hold of his arm and asked him in a low voice, 'If such women came to your house in London, what would you say?'

'Ah,' he said, and stared discomfited ahead of him.

'What are you tarts doing in my house,' she whispered. 'Isn't that what you would say?'

'Certainly not,' he hissed. 'What do you take me for?'

Looking about him he was surprised to see how diminished in numbers the party had become. The President wallah and his Amazon women were sitting on the back row with Enid and Mr Karlovitch. Bernard was alone, several rows forward, his feet propped up on the seat in front of him. The rest of the group had disappeared.

'What do you think?' persisted Olga Fiodorovna. 'They wear too much make-up, yes? Overdone, you think? They are like something by Edward Burra, by George Gross?'

'Perhaps a little,' he conceded. He couldn't understand what she was talking about.

'What do you think of the skirts, Mr Douglas?' She was pinching his arm quite severely.

'A little old-fashioned, maybe,' he said. The lights went out. They watched a film about a young girl who married a soldier. It was the old days. There was a villager who wasn't quite an idiot, more of a poet, who wandered about the fields with children following him as though he were the Pied Piper. The young girl was in love with someone else. She met him several times in secret. Her mother-in-law knew what was going on. There were many shots of poppies blowing in cornfields.

In the interval the reels had to be changed. Mr Karlovitch himself was dispatched to the projection room. Ashburner went in search of a lavatory.

He was followed by the President who, when they came to the front entrance, indicated that he should come outside.

'I need the lavatory,' explained Ashburner, tapping himself discreetly.

The President tried to take hold of his arm, but he backed away, smiling.

'I'm afraid it's urgent,' he said. 'But I'd love to come for a stroll later.'

The President shrugged his shoulders and pointed at a door along the corridor.

Ashburner entered a room divided into cubicles. Bags of cement lay mouldering in a corner. The walls and ceiling appeared to be splashed with brown paint. Opening the door of the nearest cubicle, he was faced with a cone-shaped mound of concrete cut with rough foot-holds. Climbing as best he could he rose above the level of the cubicle door and relieved himself into a hole bored into the cone. It was only when sliding down again that he realised the brown paint was excrement. He couldn't think how it had been managed. It was true that the lavatory was unnecessarily primitive in style, but even if it had been used by successive gangs of construction workers caught on the hop with upset tummies it was difficult to account for the smears on the ceiling. No wonder one picks up infections, he thought. Shaken, he went out into the passage. As he reached the front entrance a dog trotted in through the open doors and ran round his legs in a friendly fashion. He bent down and played with its ears; the dog was rather like his own, though livelier. It ran off almost immediately and he went after it to the door. It wasn't quite dark, and he could see, beyond the concrete slabs and the bulldozers, the tall figure of the President in his luminous mackintosh, standing in the road beside the parked cars,

133

talking to someone. Ashburner returned to his seat in the cinema. Bernard had fallen asleep.

'Do you think such women as those understand what they are seeing?' asked Olga Fiodorovna, stealing glances at the Amazons in the back row. 'Do you think they have brains beneath those curls?'

'I really don't know those ladies,' Ashburner protested.

'I am merely trying to find out if you have preconceived ideas,' whispered Olga Fiodorovna. 'They are both professors.'

In the second half of the film the young girl was betrayed by her mother-in-law, but not before the poetic villager had sent some sort of note to the husband telling him of his wife's assignations. At the very end the girl was dragged through the mud by neighbours and stoned to death on a hillside. When the lights came on Enid could be seen wiping her eyes with a handkerchief.

Arriving back at the hotel Ashburner was all for slipping off to bed, but surprisingly Olga Fiodorovna wouldn't hear of it. She stood arm in arm with one of the Amazon women. The President hadn't returned to the cinema after the interval and at some point before the end of the performance his other lady companion had disappeared. In the restaurant, seated by the picture window, Olga Fiodorovna still held on to the arm of her new-found friend. It seemed to Ashburner that she deliberately sat as close to her as possible, so that he would make comparisons between them. As it happened, he found the strange lady rather pleasant. Though larger than was usual, with arms like a stevedore, she was considerably less tiring to converse with than the interpreter and spoke English almost as well. She was obviously interested in him. She asked him what he did for a living.

'Well,' he said, 'I'm an Admiralty lawyer.'

'Do you enjoy your work?' she asked.

'Yes,' he said. 'I'm good at it.'

'Describe something of it to me,' she said. 'So that I will understand.'

He recounted to her the details of a case in which he had been involved for several years. A Greek American family had bought a ship which they had subsequently chartered out to an Iranian concern. The captain was a brother-in-law of the owners and took half shares in any cargo. He began to realise that pilfering was going on, on a vast scale. He was originally tipped off by the third mate, a Greek born and bred in Birmingham. 'To make matters more confusing,' Ashburner explained, 'they all had the same name – the shipping firm, the captain and the third mate. You know how it is with Greeks. They're a little like you lot with your Valentinas and Tatianas. The ship was impounded in American waters while the captain was in London. We finally took all the relevant papers to the Fraud Squad at Scotland Yard. To cut a long story short, they found there was no case.' He stopped, worried lest he was boring her. Olga Fiodorovna had already moved away and was now sitting between Bernard and Enid.

'Why?' the woman asked.

For a moment he hesitated. He wasn't sure if the name was one to bandy about in a communist country. 'The fellow that ran the Iranian concern was brother-in-law to the Shah,' he said. Now that he had got started he wanted to tell her about the trial, in particular the remark made by the third mate under cross-examination. It was perfectly suitable for an educated woman to hear. He had often told the same story at home and nobody had minded except possibly his wife. 'Funny thing happened in court,' he said. 'The third mate was asked if he was surprised at what was going on. I think I mentioned that he was born in Birmingham. "Surprised?" cried the mate. "You could have buggered me through me raincoat."'

The woman's face remained impassive. She regarded him with alarmingly bright eyes outlined in black pencil. He tried

135

to explain it to her, but he could tell she was disappointed in him. She began to discuss with Enid the meaning of the film they had watched earlier. Ashburner was taken aback to hear that the poetic villager hadn't sent a damaging note to the husband after all. It was an elaborate pretence. It suddenly struck him that it needn't have been Nina on the telephone. I have only Olga Fiodorovna's word for it, he thought. I may have been duped.

17

On their third and final day in Tblisi, Ashburner woke with swollen glands in his neck. For a moment he just lay there thinking how ill he was, and then a feeling of such unease seized him that his physical discomfort was forgotten. He could pin nothing down. His mind, usually simple, was a confusion of dark and intangible thoughts. Staggering from his bed to go into the bathroom he became aware that he was actually looking over his shoulder. He telephoned Bernard's room but received no reply. Recklessly, he rang Enid. 'I'm not awfully well,' he croaked. 'My head hurts.'

'I'm sorry,' she said. 'Do you want me to get you anything?'

'I rather wanted to speak to Bernard.'

'Well, he's not here,' Enid said, a trace sharply. 'I expect he's gone drawing. He generally goes out before breakfast. Hang on and I'll pass you some aspirins over the balcony.'

He drew back the curtains and unlocked the doors; it was another beautiful day. His eyes began to water in the sunlight. Enid's hand appeared round the side of the concrete partition holding a packet of headache powders. 'Did you lock yourself in again?' she asked. 'No wonder you feel awful.'

'Thank you,' he said, taking the powders from her. He had no intention of using them. In his weakened state he felt he needed a blood transfusion, not a few paltry grains of sodium bicarbonate.

Enid thought he was a peculiarly insecure man, always

seeking attention one way or another. In that sense he was very like Nina, though usually she chose men who looked important. Whenever Nina came to receptions or gallery openings she was accompanied by someone special, someone high up in medicine or politics. Once, at a do at the Tate, she'd brought the Russian cultural attaché – at least she'd said he was the cultural attaché: he was certainly Russian. Douglas was a nice man, even lovable, but then Nina wasn't the sort to like lovable men. Perhaps Douglas had hidden depths.

She began to laugh. 'I'm not laughing at you,' she called. 'I'm thinking of you locking yourself in. Bernard told me what happened on the train. I hope you don't think it was me?'

'Good Lord, no,' he cried, and hastily withdrew into his room.

He had locked the doors last night on account of the noise, and even then he had been unable to shut out the dull thuds and the high shivering vibrations, the footsteps that pounded along the corridor, the melancholy voices in the restaurant below droning like the wind flowing through a tunnel, raised in a Georgian chant. The singing had raged into the small hours. Once he thought he had heard Olga Fiodorovna outside his door, shouting for him to come out and play.

While Ashburner was shaving, Bernard telephoned. 'I believe you were looking for me,' he said. 'What's up now?'

'I've got an awfully sore throat,' Ashburner said.

'Fascinating,' said Bernard. 'Thanks for telling me.'

'I wondered if it was to be expected?'

'Oh,' said Bernard. 'You've started taking the pills?'

'Not yet,' Ashburner admitted. 'I didn't think it wise. Not when we keep having all this drink flung at us.'

'Then it's probably a cold,' said Bernard. 'It's the sudden change in temperature.'

'But my glands are up,' protested Ashburner. 'And I feel odd ... in my mind.'

138

'Bloody hell,' Bernard shouted. 'It's a mild infection. You're not in the final stages of syphilis.'

At breakfast, however, seeing that Ashburner did indeed look ill, sitting by the picture window hardly touching his yoghourt and dejectedly shielding his eyes from the glare of the sun, he told Olga Fiodorovna that perhaps she should take him to a doctor.

She studied Ashburner for a moment and said she didn't think it was necessary.

'It could be the beginnings of pneumonia,' Bernard warned.

'These days,' Olga Fiodorovna said, 'doctors are useless. He will either refer him to a hospital or hand him a prescription. It will save time if we go straight to the pharmacy. I know the people in charge.'

Though taking no part in the discussion on his health, Ashburner was listening. In the circumstances he thought the interpreter's attitude strange. Nina hadn't even been running a temperature and they hadn't thought twice about rushing her off in the middle of the night to a sanatorium.

'In my father's time,' reminisced Mr Karlovitch, 'there was an old man of the village. He cured everything from in-growing toenails to tumours.'

'I remember breaking my leg on a bloody railway line,' said Bernard. 'The doctor set it and put it in plaster. But that was the past, wasn't it?'

'In the past,' said Enid, 'one always went to the doctor. Never to the hospital.'

This constant reference to the past bewildered Ashburner. Squinting down at the blurred town he had the curious notion he hadn't got one.

The President sent a car for them after breakfast. They were going to ⁀ori to visit the house in which Stalin had been born. The President himself was busy but he would join them in the evening. First they must take Ashburner to the pharmacy.

Ashburner and Olga Fiodorovna disembarked on to the

road in front of a blue distempered house. On the flat roof a goat stood tethered to the chimney. Olga Fiodorovna led the way through a dark and empty shop into a storeroom at the back. The door, propped open, looked out on to a yard in which hens stalked between petrol drums. Nobody was about.

'I had a most interesting talk with your friend in the night,' said Olga Fiodorovna.

'My friend?' he said, startled.

'The President's woman,' said Olga. 'She is very clever, I think.'

'I thought she was awfully nice,' said Ashburner. He noticed that a quantity of straw quivered on the dusty floor. Overhead the goat dragged its rope across the asbestos roof. He couldn't help wondering whether he had been brought to a vet, either by mistake or design.

'She was interested to know your opinion of her, Mr Douglas.'

'Really,' he said. He was pleased.

'I told her you thought her clothing old-fashioned and her make-up too strong,' said Olga Fiodorovna.

Just then a brown hen ran in from the yard, followed by a quartet of matronly women in white coats. Olga spoke to them. Ashburner imagined that she implied he was malingering, because they looked at him without sympathy and brusquely pushed him down into a sitting position on an upturned packing case. Olga ordered him to remove his tie and unbutton his shirt. She joined in the examination of his ears and tongue. Trodden on, the hen flew squawking on to a shelf. If I am asked to take anything else off, Ashburner thought, I'll pretend I don't understand. He couldn't help comparing unfavourably this assault of farmyard women with that of a lady dentist last year, who, called in as a locum while the regular man was away, had tilted him backwards in the chair and expored the moist lining of his open, lascivious mouth with fingers fragrant with the scent of sandalwood.

140

After a noisy consultation Olga informed him there was nothing wrong apart from a mild inflammation of the throat. He was handed a cup of water and three differently coloured capsules. Obediently he swallowed the pills and put a further supply, neatly packaged in blue paper, into the pocket of his coat. He had hardly taken a few paces through the shop when he was afflicted with a curious sensation of weightlessness. Foolishly smiling, he floated through the door. The road swirled beneath him, striped with sunshine, dappled with leaves. He had to be hauled down like a flag to fit inside the car. He fell instantly asleep with his head on Enid's shoulder.

Presently he awoke and found himself alone with Bernard in a parked car in a village square. Outside stood Olga Fiodorovna, arm in arm with Mr Karlovitch, looking up at a war memorial. At a distance a little child in a black dress crouched on the cobblestones, staring at the car. There was no sign of Enid or the driver.

'All right then, mate?' asked Bernard.

'Fine,' said Ashburner. He did feel well, though less affable now that he had come down to earth. 'Is this it?' he asked.

'No,' said Bernard. 'Enid wanted to pee.'

'Aren't you going to stretch your legs?' said Ashburner.

'There's nothing here that interests me,' said Bernard.

Ashburner left the car and called out to Mr Karlovitch and the interpreter. The child ran headlong across the square and into a doorway. Olga Fiodorovna turned and stared at Ashburner as if she didn't know who he was; he had the dark thought that she hadn't expected to see him on his feet. Reaching her and respectfully bowing his head in the shadow of the war memorial, he asked in a low voice if there wasn't some little café they could pop into for a morning drink of coffee. 'It is morning, isn't it?' he enquired, not sure how long he had slept.

Mr Karlovitch said certainly it was morning but it was a little early for drinking, even for him. They would drink themselves under the table at Gori.

Appalled at such a prospect, Ashburner sauntered away and came to a little path bordered with wild raspberries that led to an ancient church glimpsed through eucalyptus trees. As he walked he whistled, not wishing to embarrass Enid should she be squatting in the bushes. He didn't look up; he was thinking of yesterday and wondering if his liver hadn't been permanently damaged. The President had taken them to a dusty plateau on a hillside to the south of Tblisi. Honoured guests at a Fair, they had stumbled from tent to tent, from enclosure to encampment. Forced to sit on upturned buckets in front of fiercely glowing wood fires, various friends of the President had pressed them to sample the young wine and the old. Whether under canvas or the blue sky, a goggling populace had observed their every move, separated from the inner sanctum by barricades. At some point a cookery demonstration had taken place. Men with daggers in their belts stood over vats of semolina and alternatively whipped and stirred the glutinous mess with paddles. A boy, stripped to the waist, worked the bellows against the fire. They had all broken down, weeping from the smoke. The crowd, lips bursting open like plums, swayed against the barricades and split their sides with laughter. Bernard was photographed amid a wedding party from Tashkent. Placed incongruously between the groom, who wore white, and a fat girl in a navy blue anorak, he smirked uncertainly into the camera. Behind him stood a row of octogenarian giants in astrakhan caps, mouths inlaid with teeth of solid gold. As the shutter clicked, the golden, flash-bulb smiles exploded in the sunlight.

In all that wine-consuming day, bloated with semolina pudding, garlanded with pink carnations and laden with gifts, grapes, honey sticks, handkerchieves from Samarkand, no one mentioned Nina. Not once. When they returned to Moscow, thought Ashburner, she would always be about to arrive, or have just left.

142

Turning a bend in the path he saw Enid, standing on tiptoe at a wire fence, peeping in a furtive manner at something beyond. At his approach she looked over her shoulder and gestured for him to keep quiet. He stood stock still on the path.

'What's up?' he whispered.

She beckoned him and he stared through the netting at a vegetable garden filled with runner beans in flower.

'It's Rasputin,' she said. 'I've just seen Rasputin.' Behind a wall of green leaves a man moved slowly up and down, snipping with secateurs. 'Look at his beard,' she hissed. 'Look at his eyes.' But dazzled by the sunshine Ashburner saw nothing save a figure in a long black coat.

In the car, Enid described what she had seen. She was full of it. 'There were several men at one time,' she cried, 'planting things. One of them threw a dead sheep over the wall. A man and a dog were passing and the dog sniffed at the sheep and Rasputin threw a stone at the dog to make it leave off.

'What sort of a dog?' asked Olga Fiodorovna. Ashburner noticed that Mr Karlovitch was looking at her in the driving mirror. He was frowning.

'Just a dog,' said Enid. 'The man had a long beard, didn't he?' She appealed to Ashburner.

'I'm afraid I didn't see anything like that,' he confessed. 'But then I'm not very observant, and of course I've been recently drugged.' He hadn't meant to sound quite so censorious.

'Such eyes,' exclaimed Enid. 'Like Indian ink. And hair right down to his shoulders.'

'Monks,' said Olga Fiodorovna. 'Georgia is full of monasteries.'

Bernard was staggered. He had thought religion stamped out and all the priests sent packing to Siberia. He could have kicked himself for having remained in the car and missed those hippie monks.

143

'This is not Moscow,' said Mr Karlovitch. 'Nobody cares. The churches are empty.'

'They're giving away the ikons to every Tom, Dick and Harry,' remarked Ashburner, remembering his conversation with Tatiana's husband in the forest.

They arrived in Gori in mid-afternoon, too late for the reception committee who had given them up for lost and gone home. The museum was heavily padlocked. Ashburner was tremendously agitated when he understood; he hated unpunctuality and felt personally responsible for the inconvenience caused. He squirmed at the thought of the prepared speeches unspoken, the minor officials trailing forlornly homewards with hands unshaken. 'God, how awful,' he said to Bernard. 'I feel dreadful for having wasted so much time at the chemist's.'

Seeing his perturbed, perspiring face, Mr Karlovitch asked if he was unwell again.

'Believe me, I had no idea,' protested Ashburner incoherently. 'If only I had known.'

'There's nothing wrong with him,' said Bernard. 'Nothing medical anyway.' Looking out at the petrol station, the combine harvesters, the rows of ugly shops, he wondered why he had been so anxious to come.

Olga Fiodorovna went off to find somebody important who might have a key to the museum. The others left the car and strolled up and down a withered strip of grass beside the main road. On the opposite side of the street a group of sailors stood drunkenly arguing beneath a tattered tree. Ashburner was shocked at the sight, though relieved to know that the Russian navy was no different from anyone else's. Even so, he turned round and pretended to be studying a concrete horse trough dug into the ground; he imagined that Mr Karlovitch must be feeling pretty hot under the collar. In his head, he told a gathering of impressed colleagues how in Georgia he had witnessed at first hand the undisciplined behaviour of Soviet

144

sailors, and then he remembered he couldn't tell anyone. He was supposed to be fishing in Scotland. He wondered if he could transpose the incident to Scapa Flow.

After half an hour Olga Fiodorovna returned with the Major, the lady curator of the Museum and a man in dirty overalls who wasn't introduced.

'I'm frightfully sorry,' said Ashburner, wringing the Mayor's hand and casting sorrowful glances at the lady curator.

Nobody else apologised. They crossed the road and walked up a dilapidated side street until they came to a stretch of open ground on which stood a statue of Karl Marx, a Greek temple on legs and a red brick building fronted with stained glass windows.

'Flipping hell,' said Bernard.

Stalin's house lay under the temple. It was a mud hut arrangement, obviously reinforced by modern methods, comprising one room and a cellar. A stove pipe was sticking out of the roof. There was a rocking chair, a bed with a spotless white counterpane and a framed photograph on the wall of Stalin as a child, set between his mother and father.

Enid said he looked beautiful – a bit like Omar Sharif without the moustache. 'Such eyes,' she cried, and thought again of the monk in the bean garden.

Bernard was disappointed. He had expected to feel something. It was that bloody silly Greek temple that ruined everything. He started to go down into the cellar, but the curator took hold of his sleeve and restrained him. He stood in the doorway and wondered what she would do if he lay down on the bed.

'You must know,' said the curator, speaking in a curiously Australian accent, 'that it was here that the young child was born to poor but honest peasants. Notice the bed, notice the floor.'

She was looking sternly at Ashburner.

'His mother was a half-wit,' said Bernard, nudging Ashburner in the back. 'And his old man an alcoholic.'

'It's all so fascinating,' Ashburner said. 'Quite remarkable.'

They weren't allowed to descend into the cellar. No explanation was given. Fuming, Bernard was led away.

'Why can't we?' he muttered, pestering Olga Fiodorovna.

'Mr Burns,' she said reasonably, 'what's so marvellous about a hole in the ground?'

When they entered the museum the curator wanted it to be understood that only two rooms were open for inspection. 'You must know,' she told them, 'that we are renovating the rest of the exhibition.'

'Revamping, she means,' Bernard said. 'They're wiping out any reference to anything after 1945.'

The largest of the two rooms were filled mainly with photographs and tracts. A glass case displayed Stalin's school reports and various essays he had written as a brilliant schoolboy. Everyone except Bernard pretended to be interested in the reports and crowded round the cabinet with murmurs of awed appreciation. They must know, the lady curator drawled, that as a child Stalin had been known as Zo-Zo. Zo-Zo had written many gifted poems.

At the other end of the room Bernard was stomping up and down, looking at the photographs and snorting with contempt. 'Where is Voroshilov?' he suddenly shouted. 'And Marshall Blucher and Kamenev? Where is Comrade Trotsky?'

Everyone ignored him, though Ashburner grew very red in the face.

'What do you think of her?' asked Olga Fiodorovna, linking arms with him and staring critically at the curator. 'She is no good at her job, yes? You like her legs?'

'For heaven's sake,' said Ashburner crossly. 'I'm not a womaniser.'

There wasn't time to take it all in. The curator was

146

obviously in a hurry; she ran her visitors round the room and out through the door as if the building had caught fire behind them. The smaller room contained more photographs, more reports and articles, this time from Bolshevik newspapers. In a corner stood a statue of Lenin with a marble cap on his head.

'You must know,' informed the curator, 'that Stalin was revolting from 1898 onwards. At the age of nineteen he became one of the founders of the Tiflis branch of the Social Democratic Workers' Party.'

'Are there any paintings we can look at?' enquired Bernard grimly. Answering himself, he cried out uncontrollably, 'Any paintings? What a bloody daft idea. What would a load of artists be doing looking at paintings?' He limped ferociously across the room and out of the door and could be heard pattering down the stairs in his plimsolls.

Ashburner followed a few moments later. He was worried lest Bernard had gone overboard and was now running amok in the town, possibly brawling with the inebriated sailors. Peering over the banisters he saw him standing in the hall below with the Mayor and the man in the mucky overalls. For a fraction of a second he imagined he heard Bernard speaking in Russian. Clattering down the stairs, he called out, 'Everything all right?'

'Hunky dory,' said Bernard. 'I was just telling these blokes here that Zo-Zo's Dad was a boozer.'

18

They had lunch at the People's Palace in the main street. Many strangers drank to their health, to the loved ones they had left behind and to their safe return to Moscow. Bernard went so far as to raise his glass to Stalin. It went down very well. According to the Mayor, Stalin was returning to favour among the younger generation. The young were becoming increasingly romantic about the past and puritanical about the present.

'I know what you mean,' cried Bernard, and he launched into a rambling speech that dealt with falling standards in architecture, and the lack of corner shops and the absence of friendly policemen.

Assessing his condition, Olga Fiodorovna gradually stopped translating his remarks. She told Enid and Ashburner to eat up their food. 'The cooking ladies have gone to a lot of trouble,' she scolded. 'You will offend them.' Relentlessly she heaped meat and chips and bread stuffed with cabbage leaves on to their plates.

Enid wore a shoulder bag slung from her neck like a bus conductress. The bag was deep and contained nothing but an unposted letter to her mother and a comb. When no one was looking she shovelled the remainder of her food, and Ashburner's, into this convenient receptacle.

'Knock down the bloody buildings,' Bernard was shouting. 'And you wipe away the past.' He waved his knife in the air, indicating the cracked ceiling above them, the cobwebbed cornices, the stained and peeling walls. 'Only think,' he said. 'Perhaps in this very room Uncle Joe paced the floor, spoke, put his fingerprints on the door handle.'

'This building is five years old,' commented Olga Fiodorovna.

It didn't matter to Bernard. 'One day,' he said, sitting down and leaning confidentially towards Ashburner, 'one day they'll invent a machine to pick up all the conversations left wandering about with nowhere to go.' He stared at a crack in the ceiling as though he saw lost words clustered like flies.

Before they rose from the table Enid complained that she felt cold. Gallantly Mr Karlovitch lent her his coat. When they went outside into the street Ashburner was astonished at the prominence of her stomach. Someone took a photograph of the group, posed against the door of the People's Palace. Enid was in the centre, her swollen handbag hidden beneath Mr Karlovitch's coat. 'Mother Enid,' cried the Mayor, kissing her farewell on both cheeks.

They left Gori at six o'clock. The sky had turned green and it was raining heavily. Even Olga Fiodorovna fell asleep. Only Ashburner and the driver remained awake. Ashburner wished he had shone a little more at the luncheon. Perhaps nobody would remember that he had ever been there. Certainly he had never raised his voice. He remembered Nina's last words to him, spoken outside the lift in the Peking Hotel. 'I'm not promising,' she had said, 'but I may come to your room.' When I'm dead, he thought, and Bernard's machine has been invented, no one will know what she meant.

They had been driving for two hours through flat countryside, the rain continuously falling, when the car began to slow down. Ahead of them waited a sinister black limousine. Suddenly a man jumped out into the road and ran towards them.

'Good Lord,' cried Ashburner, 'It's what's-his-name.'

149

He shook Olga Fiodorovna, who woke and poked her head irritably out of the window. Seeing the President of the Tblisi Artists' Union standing out there in the rain, she smiled. After a brief exchange he ran back to the limousine and drove off. The car reversed and followed, driving along a winding lane between potato fields.

'We are going to a special monastery in the mountains,' explained Olga Fiodorovna. 'Mr Burns will be pleased.'

It took some time to reach the mountains and still longer to find the exact route to the monastery. It was growing dark. They climbed steeply, swaying over pot-holes and throwing up cascades of muddy water which dashed against the windows of the car. The driver swore often.

Bernard woke groaning. He thought he was in an aeroplane, caught in air turbulence. 'This isn't doing my hip any good,' he complained, lighting himself a cigarette. Had Olga Fiodorovna protested he would have throttled her.

They arrived eventually in a gloomy village surrounded by pine trees. The driver sounded his horn and an old man came blinking into the headlamps of the car. Instructed by the President, he tottered off into the trees and presently returned with a lumpy boy who was wearing oil-skins and carrying a bunch of keys. The cars could go no further. Everyone was told to get out. Ashburner was relieved to see that the President was accompanied by three members of his committee and hadn't brought the Amazon women. Olga Fiodorovna stayed in the car. She had seen it all before.

They toiled up a steep slope, the boy bounding ahead, leaping over boulders and jangling his keys.

'Do you need a hand?' asked Ashburner, concerned that Bernard might stumble and fall.

'Get off,' said Bernard, head bent against the driving rain. His trousers were soaked through. 'It had better be good,' he added in a threatening tone, as though it was Ashburner who had devised such a perilous outing.

150

When they reached the top of the slope it was too dark to see the monastery. All they could discern was a blackened shape towering against the stormy sky. They heard the boy unlock the door and then scuffling sounds and a little echoing yelp of pain.

'He is looking for the lights,' said Mr Karlovitch. 'Many tourists come here. It is an attraction.'

'I think I can see a bit of battlement,' cried Ashburner, and he moved a few paces to his left.

'Do not stray, Mr Douglas,' cautioned Mr Karlovitch. 'We are standing on a cliff above a ravine.'

It appeared there was something wrong with the electricity supply; the President and his retinue stumbled after the boy.

'I'm cold, Vladimir,' whimpered Enid, as though about to recite an epic poem.

Mr Karlovitch guided his drenched visitors to the door. 'Do not worry,' he comforted them; 'there are no steps', and tripping over a length of cable he struck his head on a stone. Shouting blasphemously, the President and his men roamed the sooty darkness until, striking matches and lighters, they feebly illuminated a small circle of floor strewn with building materials.

'Perhaps there's a candle,' said Bernard, and he began to strike his own matches and gradually lit his way to some stone steps. He sat down and took out another cigarette.

'We are in a place founded in the eleventh century,' Mr Karlovitch said. 'Before that it was also here, but the Arabs destroyed it. However, stones remain from the fourth century and are still in peak condition.' His face, glimpsed briefly in the flare of a match, was ashen; a trickle of blood ran down his left cheek.

Ashburner stood with his back to a crumbling wall, his arms stretched out on either side to anchor himself. The blackness under which he was crushed was interfering with his sense of balance. He felt as though he was swaying on a

151

windowsill at the top of the Empire State building. I'm perfectly all right, he told himself. I am among friends. But in fact he was beginning to experience that same catatonic state of helplessness which had seized him on the bridge at Leningrad. For an instant he saw the white sleeve of the President's mackintosh raised above the head of the mountain boy who was kneeling on the floor, recklessly fiddling with electric wires.

Then someone thrust a lighter into Ashburner's hand. Making a tremendous effort he flicked the flint, and as the spark caught the petrol and the small flame leapt he saw Nina, her face and shoulders not a yard from him, her eyes looking at him with such an expression of entreaty and desperation that he let fall the lighter. At the same moment the electricity came on; he found he was facing Enid who also looked at him, her mouth open in shock. 'Nina was here,' he said. He sank downwards until he sat on the floor with his legs stretched out.

Enid believed him. She wanted to run and tell Bernard, but she thought Ashburner might think she was trying to cash in on his own personal, supernatural revelation. She squatted down in front of him, the skirt of her pink frock tight over her splayed knees. 'What did she want?' she asked, and felt immediately foolish. Already she didn't believe him.

'Nothing,' Ashburner said. 'It's too late. Someone hit her over the head at that studio by the lake. I've always known it. Petrov knew it too. So did his wife. They put a rug down because the floor was stained.'

Enid was alarmed. She nodded sympathetically and taking her time stood up and sauntered across to Bernard who was sitting on the altar steps. 'It's got something, this place,' he said, staring at a vast and ruined arch which vaulted into the shadows.

'Douglas ought to be taken back to the hotel,' said Enid. 'He's gone really peculiar now. He thinks Nina's been murdered.'

152

'I know,' said Bernard.

'Where is Nina?' asked Enid.

'She's probably back in London,' Bernard said. 'She got cold feet, didn't she? She never could follow anything through.'

'He's wracked,' whispered Enid, looking at Ashburner. 'Wracked.'

'Of course he is,' said Bernard. 'The poor sod's in love. He thinks that when she walks the world holds up its head.'

They both fell silent, a bit put out, and stole glances at the fortunate Ashburner sat slumped against the wall, blessed with visions, tormented by demons. Neither of them could think how Ashburner had stumbled on the art of loving; love depended on the ability to like oneself and required an understanding of eternal regret.

'He didn't seem the type,' said Enid, at last. Remembering his ineptness on the midnight express when she had mistaken him for Mr Karlovitch, she wondered if the fault lay in herself.

19

They flew back to Moscow late the next day and had a restrained farewell dinner in the restaurant of the Peking Hotel. Enid presented both Olga Fiodorovna and Mr Karlovitch with numerous pairs of nylon stockings. Ashburner had purchased the extra large size by mistake. 'I'm frightfully sorry,' he said. 'I'm not much good at shopping.'

Olga Fiodorovna said they wouldn't be wasted; perhaps she would post them on to his lady friend in Tblisi. When the band struck up she danced with Bernard.

'I really like you,' he said. 'As soon as I get home, I'll write you a letter.'

'But of course,' she replied, without rancour, and, smiling, foxtrotted beneath the Chinese lanterns.

In the lobby, before he went upstairs, she told Ashburner that Mrs St Clair would join them after breakfast and travel to the airport in the official car.

'How nice,' he said, and stepped into the lift.

Packing his suitcase the following morning, Ashburner remembered the shirt loaned to him by Boris's friend Tatiana. It was simply not on to take it home with him, torn or otherwise. He took out the paper bag Tatiana had given him and removing his own shirt replaced it with the borrowed one. He threw the bag carelessly on to a chair. After locking his suitcase he looked round for his fishing rod. It was missing. He

154

had last seen it at the airport at Tblisi. Bernard had insisted on carrying it. He had turned on the steps of the aircraft and held it aloft in a final salute to the President and his committee.

Ashburner was about to leave the room – he had tucked the paper bag under his arm thinking he would hand it over to Olga Fiodorovna – when he noticed a scrap of paper lying on the floor. It had obviously fallen from the folds of his shirt. He picked it up and read the words 'Dzerzhinsky Square', followed by the number 827. It was simply an address, nothing more. It was in Nina's handwriting.

He stood for some time, just holding the piece of paper, twisting it this way and that, trying to work out how it had come to be inside his shirt. Presently he came to the conclusion that it was a sign from Nina. She had instructed Boris Shabelsky to give her address to her dear friend, Douglas Ashburner. It had been that day she had set off to visit Pasternak's grave. Ill, or frightened, she had decided not to return to the Peking Hotel. He imagined her telling Boris how important it was. 'I will be safer in Dzerzhinsky Square,' she may have said. Shabelsky, Ashburner thought, had intended to hand it over personally, only that wretched business with the dog outside the bathroom window had prevented him. Later, as he was carried to the car, Tatiana had popped it into the bag along with his shirt.

Perhaps, Ashburner thought, Nina was alive after all. She was expecting him.

Downstairs in the lobby he waited with Bernard and Enid for the luggage to be put into the car. His fishing rod lay across Bernard's carrier bags. There was a delay. Either the car wasn't there or Olga Fiodorovna had mislaid an important document. She was on the telephone again, leaning against the booking desk with her back to them.

'I never sent any post-cards,' fretted Enid.

Bernard began to hum something from the opera they had

155

seen in Leningrad, some melody sung by Faustus after he had sold his soul to the Devil.

I don't have to sell anything, thought Ashburner. I have simply to go into the street.

He walked to the stacked suitcases and picked up his fishing rod. He had the idea that if Olga Fiodorovna called out to him he would pretend he was taking luggage to the car. He went out of the door into the frozen street.

The cab driver who stopped for him studied the scrap of paper and seemed not to understand.

'Dzerzhinsky Square,' said Ashburner desperately, trying his best to pronounce the name correctly. Remembering the money Olga Fiodorovna had pressed upon him, he took out the envelope containing a hundred roubles and thrust it into the driver's hand.

Ten minutes later, his fishing rod under his arm, he was walking up and down a prosperous street. He couldn't find No. 827. He stood well back in the gutter and looked up at the secretive houses. He had no notion of what he should do next. He had half expected Nina to be waiting for him – in the flesh or in the spirit. A hundred panes of shut glass reflected the whiteness of the road. Just then a window opened on the top floor of an office block. Remembering the first lines of the shameful poem dedicated to Nina, he ran up the appropriate steps and hammered on the door. He heard a dog frantically barking.

A man in horn-rimmed spectacles unzipped the canvas case and extricating the fishing rod removed the sheets of paper wrapped about its stem. The drawings of ships and docks and palaces were dampened and mounted on cardboard to be examined by experts. Meanwhile in another room another man told Ashburner to empty the contents of his pockets. He then left, locking the door behind him.

Ashburner stood beside a mahogany desk. Someone had confiscated his boots. There was no doubt in his mind that he

156

was the victim of a monstrous conspiracy. He was being used to expiate some misdemeanor, some crime perpetrated against the State. He took out his wallet, his travellers cheques, Nina's letter and the pink scarf and arranged them neatly on the desk. Olga Fiodorovna had his passport. He realised that if Bernard had been in his shoes – always supposing they hadn't been taken from him – he would have found his situation credible. He would merely put it down to an error in the computer. It was strange that Bernard, whose profession it was to arrange lumps of paint into recognisable shapes and patterns, had been unable to discern this particular composition. Ashburner himself saw the completed picture quite clearly. Unlike Nina's husband the brain specialist, he found a frame unnecessary. He perceived a man and a woman in a bleak landscape, frozen in their tracks.

Stepping to the barred window he looked down into a sunken patch of yard under snow. He still held a creased snapshot of his wife and her Uncle Robert, arm in arm in the winter garden. His wife was smiling.

Even the man who is sensible and composed, he thought, must pale before life's contradictions.